All Things Work Together

BRIGETTE MANIE

ISBN: 1499181620

ISBN-13: 9781499181623

Cover Design: ebookcoversgalore.com

Edited by Hazel McGhie

Printed in the United States of America by Createspace.com

DEDICATION

To every woman who has cared for a child, whether or not you gave birth to that child.

"You don't appear to have any experience dealing with teenagers. I have two."

His statement came out skeptical, and Jasmine took it as criticism. She felt a kick of resistance in her belly but controlled it. "This is a profession-specific resume, Pastor King. That means it's unique to teaching. If I'd had time I would have adjusted it to be more comprehensive and reflective of *all* my experiences as they relate to dealing with children." She smiled but knew from the way his right eyebrow edged towards his hairline, he'd heard the patronage that she hadn't fought too hard to camouflage. A bit of rebellion had reached the surface. Her sweet smile didn't say 'sorry,' and she did not speak that word.

"Well, Ms. Lewis," he glanced at his watch, "we have a little time now, so why don't you *enlighten* me as to how comprehensive that experience is?"

Watch it! He's a potential employer. No tit for tat here. Control your tongue. She widened her smile, took a breath, and took a shot at obedience.

TITLES BY BRIGETTE MANIE

The Banning Island Series

Against His Will

Tropical Eyewitness

Five Brothers Books

From Passion to Pleasure

Once in This Lifetime

Someone Like You

The Seneca Mountain Romances

A Fall for Grace

A Price Too High

All Things Work Together (novella)

Mahogany and Daniel

A Man Apart

Forever With You

CHAPTER I

After the broken stiletto heel, the flat tire, and "Speedy Cab" turned "Crawl Cab," she should have known the day wouldn't end well. But she'd ignored the warning signs and walked right into this. Jasmine dredged up a smile, just to be professional, and reminded the man facing her, "I have an offer of employment and follow up communication, showing acceptance of the offer. Furthermore, I have a letter stating that a contract is waiting here for my signature to officially make me the sixth grade teacher at Indian Run SAB School."

The tolerant smile of Michael Bump, new principal at Indian Run about whom she knew nothing until this moment, set her teeth on edge.

"Ms. Lewis, your resume shows that you've been with our school system for a while. Therefore, you should know that principals cannot hire teachers. Only the Superintendent of Schools can do that."

What was this flea-brained individual trying to say? Did he doubt the legitimacy of her employment? Was he saying that the super knew nothing about her? Did he think that Mrs. Yale, the principal who'd interviewed her initially, had gone vigilante in the system and was hiring people on her own? Jasmine educated him. "My application went *directly* to the Superintendent's office. *They* forwarded my resume to Mrs. Yale at Indian Run. She then interviewed me and called me for a follow up interview with the Superintendent. He did not join us physically but cleared me for hiring by phone." Jasmine didn't try to hide the hauteur in her tone;

neither did she attempt to cover the sarcasm. The man had rubbed her the wrong way with that patronizing little speech, implying she was a dunce and unaware of Second Advent Believers (SAB) Education Department's hiring rules.

"Well, Ms. Lewis, I can see you're familiar with employment procedures and practices," he said, an insincere smile slithering like slime across his stingy lips. From his manner to his appearance he was repulsive. Jasmine wanted to smack his smugness into the next century. "However, since you give attention to details, how did you not pick up that your letter of employment wasn't quite official and, therefore, not at all legitimate?"

Jasmine blinked. "Excuse me?"

He didn't try to cover his smirk of satisfaction. "This so called letter of employment confirmation that you brought," he began, tossing her letter across the desk with a disdainful flick of his wrist, "does not have the Superintendent's seal on it."

"His signature is there," she pointed out.

"Forged, which is why our dear Mrs. Yale is not here."

Jasmine started catching flies. Her mouth was that wide open.

"Ah, I see you didn't know that, eh?"

Somehow a statement that should have sounded sympathetic for her situation came out like a gloat. Jasmine closed her mouth.

"Now," the wretched man continued, "compare this letter"—he shoved a sheet of paper across his desk towards her—"to this one."

That one had a seal and while the signatures on the letters were similar, they were not mirror images of one another. One was a forgery all right. And without an official seal, it meant hers was the forgery.

"I'm sorry, Ms. Lewis," Mr. Bump said, sounding truly contrite for the first time. Maybe her shell-shocked expression had gotten to him. "I know you have travelled a great distance for employment you thought was legitimate. I regret that this has happened. Superintendent Shane would have been here today to address you personally on this matter, but he had a sudden death in the family and had to travel overseas. He has, however, given me a letter for you." He pulled out a desk drawer and extended a sealed envelope to her.

Jasmine took it, unable to contain the tremor in her hand as the implications of not getting the job slammed her. She had literally relocated from Florida and had all her furniture moved into her new apartment in the village of Indian Run. There was no home or job to go back to, no alternative, and no back-up plan. Without a job she was up a financial creek! Mr. Bump started speaking again, and Jasmine struggled to focus.

"In a nutshell, the letter apologizes for the inconvenience this forgery may have caused. Your relocation expenses will be refunded as well as any home or car rental costs you may have incurred. There's an address in the letter where you can send receipts for the same." He pushed his chair back and stood. "I know this has all been a shock for you and too much to take in, Ms. Lewis, but Mrs. Yale's dishonesty has brought all this about." He went to the door and opened it. "I hate to rush you, but I have another appointment waiting. I wish you all the best, and you may call the Superintendent's office with any questions."

Jasmine stood and turned slowly. He was in a rush to get rid of her, but something was nagging at her. "I understand about the forgery, Mr. Bump, but what about the vacancy for the sixth grade teacher? Is it not still available?"

He shook his head. "It is not."

Jasmine smelled a rat. "Has it been filled then?" she asked.

Mr. Bump looked suddenly uncomfortable and didn't meet her eyes.

Lots of rats.

"Look, Ms. Lewis, I'm just a messenger here. Like I said, you can call the Superintendent with further questions."

Jasmine's spine went erect, and she leveled her *I-don't-take-crap* stare at him. "I didn't ask you if you were a messenger, Mr. Bump. I asked if the job was filled."

"Yes," he admitted, tugging at his tie like it was choking him.

"Let me get this straight," Jasmine started, a hand moving to her hip and her tone turning combative. "I don't have a job through no fault of my own. I didn't do any forgery and bear in mind that the Superintendent verbally offered me the job before the alleged forgery. Yet said job was given to someone else. There's something very wrong with this picture."

Mr. Bump was sweating now. He mopped his brow with a handkerchief. "Ms. Lewis, I'm just an intermediary delivering a message. Please call the Superintendent if you have doubts and objections to the rescinding of the employment offer."

"Oh, I have lots of objections and a great deal of doubt about the legitimacy and the ethics, or rather the lack of ethics, involved in withdrawal of my job offer. I need to register my concerns today. How can I reach the Superintendent abroad?"

"He's not reachable." His eyes had gone shifty again. Jasmine didn't believe him.

"He's the head of a whole school system. You must have a cell or land line overseas for him. I suggest you find a number and give it to me before this reaches the New York State Labor board."

That threat garnered some quick cooperation. Bump hurried back to his desk and dialed a number. He put the phone on speaker and motioned her closer.

I should have applied to the public school district, Jasmine thought while the phone rang. She was tired of the foolishness in the SAB school system. It had been especially bad this past year, her final year with the SAB School in Ft Lauderdale, Florida. She had a strong feeling that she was a victim of the foolishness and politics that were pervasive in SAB education. More than likely her job had been given to some relative or friend of the Superintendent. Mrs. Yale's so called forgery had been a convenient excuse not only to get rid of the woman but also the candidate that she had selected with the Superintendent's approval. Jasmine was convinced of the correctness of her conclusion the more she thought on the matter. Why else would they not hire her? She had done nothing wrong. She wasn't guilty of anything. So why was she paying? Why didn't she have a job?

"Robert Shane."

This man could answer her questions.

"Superintendent Shane, this is Jasmine Lewis, the lady whose employment offer was rescinded at Indian Run School."

***

By the time she got off the phone Jasmine was angry. Superintendent Shane had been polite at first, but by the end of the conversation he had become cold and dismissive. He said they didn't hire her because they no longer had confidence in the choice of a known forger. Hence they had hired another teacher. Jasmine pointed out that it wasn't professional or Christian to persecute her for someone else's wrong. He'd gotten chilly after that statement, saying that he took his Christianity seriously and didn't appreciate her impugning it or his character. A decision had been made, the job was no longer available, and she could send moving receipts to his office. With a firm 'good day,' he hung up.

She closed her eyes for a brief moment, exhaled agitation, and pulled herself together. She had sustained a more gigantic blow in life and had survived. She would make it through this too. The divorce had been far worse than this. Straightening her shoulders and her spine, she stepped with confidence she didn't feel to the door. She shook the hand Bump offered and even managed to return his snarky smile with a professional lift of her lips. Then she kept her head straight and walked away from the second major disaster in her life experience.

***

Jasmine watched the sunrise from the porch of her new apartment on Cherry Drive in the village of Indian Run. At nearly eight o'clock on this Tuesday morning in August, the breeze blew strong and brisk, shaking the leaves of the maple tree across the way, and tossing strands of her flat-ironed black hair across her face. She liked watching the sun come up. It spoke of new birth and brought with it possibilities that yesterday's experience had dulled into disbelief.

The stove in the apartment wasn't working. Maintenance promised to come around noon to fix it. In the meantime, she needed a cup of tea and some breakfast. An electric kettle would come in handy, but since she didn't have one, a trip into the village was her alternative. There had to be breakfast shops. Every town big or small had them.

Jasmine dragged on jeans, dropped a T-shirt over her head and stepped into her sneakers. She grabbed a light jacket on her way out the door. The road sloped towards the village. Jasmine kept to the sidewalk and inhaled the freshness of the mountain air as she trekked downhill. Two squirrels darted in front of her, making her jump, and then scrambled up the trunk of a hemlock, chasing each other in a spiral pattern.

At the foot of the hill, she waited to cross to the other side of Main Street as morning commuters whizzed by. When the light changed, she stepped onto the crosswalk, headed with eagerness for The Breakfast Shop. Everything and everyone it seemed was on the

5

internet these days. She'd googled dining in Indian Run, New York and had come up with a list of restaurants. The Breakfast Shop catered to vegetarians. She was vegan. There had to be something she could eat there.

***

In the final months of her marriage, Jasmine had accepted the inevitability of divorce. She understood that her marriage was a train barreling towards wreckage that she couldn't stop because she needed help to avert the disaster. Her partner, soon to be ex-husband, didn't want to help her. Simon was the problem to start with. And frankly, she didn't want to avert disaster. It wasn't salvageable when not only had he cheated on her but he'd also knocked up the girl—gotten her pregnant—and took it further by setting her up in an apartment and moving in with her. Worrying was not going to change the outcome of the marriage; so why add more stress to her life by indulging in a useless exercise?

Now, she was out of a job—in a brand new town where she knew no one, and where she had no prospects or connections to secure employment. The outlook was bleak, just like life without Simon had once looked. Two years later she was still a survivor. Like her divorce and the pain of it, this joblessness too shall pass, she told herself. God said to cast all her cares on Him. She'd spent a good portion of last night doing that.

As she sat at an outdoor table before The Breakfast Shop in Indian Run's tiny village, Jasmine wasn't about to pick up those cares again. Being a problem solver though, she wondered what she was going to do. She had paid one month's rent and one month's security, so she could live in her two bedroom apartment rent free for the next four weeks. She had to get a job soon. Her cash supply plus what she had in the bank amounted to about $5,000. How long would that last with an $800 per month rent plus other expenses? Not long.

Jasmine blew air into the cup of mint tea and watched a candy wrapper tumbling across the square, a slight wind giving lazy pursuit. Business began slowly, it seemed, in this small town. Closed signs still hung in most store windows and at entrance doors to shops. Across the street Sasha's Style, a boutique advertising designer wear at thrift shop prices, opened for business. Frank's Donuts and Bagel Shop had been open when she arrived this morning. Roswell Bank, the one locally owned bank still operating in the town, opened at seven o'clock. Maybe that's how they stayed in business, keeping longer hours than their competitors. Main, the street found in every city in America, ran through the town square. The traffic volume started picking up. A UPS truck sped by followed by an eighteen wheeler.

Jasmine finished her tea and the scrambled tofu sandwich she'd ordered from The Breakfast Shop. Her phone rang as she pushed away from the table. She glanced at the screen: Her mother.

"Hi, mom, how's everything?"

"Everything's wonderful, honey. And in a minute you'll think so too." Acquilla Lewis was usually cheerful, but she sounded a little excited right now.

The vibrant and energetic greeting had Jasmine smiling. "What's going on mom?"

"I think I have a job for you."

"Really? What?" Jasmine asked, very interested now.

"After you told me what happened with the job yesterday, I went to dinner with Jim last night and met an old friend at the restaurant we went to. It just so happens that her son needs a babysitter-chaperone for his kids right now. It pays two thousand a month without room and board and fifteen hundred if room and board have to be provided."

Jasmine stopped listening and did some quick mental math. If she took the room and board, she could save three hundred on rent. If she didn't, her monthly salary would be only $1,300 after paying an $800 rent.

"How old are the children?" she asked her mother.

"I just told you." Acquilla sounded like she was frowning.

"Sorry. My mind wandered a bit."

"Sixteen, fourteen, and ten."

"I thought you said there were four children."

"There are. The last two are twins. Are you interested?"

"I am. When can I meet your friend's son?"

"Today, if Norma and I can arrange it. He's right there in Mohawk Valley, only thirty minutes from you."

Mohawk Valley was one of the four communities that comprised the Seneca Mountain Area along with Indian Run, Heart Haven, and Mountain Spring.

"Okay, so you'll call me back with a time and place?" Jasmine asked her mother.

"I will. Talk to you later."

Jasmine disconnected with a smile, thinking God is good all the time. What did He say in Isaiah 30:19? While His children are seeking solutions in prayer, He provides an answer. She picked up her teacup and headed into The Breakfast Shop humming "My God is Awesome."

***

"Mom, this isn't a good idea," Adam King protested as he exited The Family Care Group, the agency where he worked as a counselor three times per week.

"Unless you have a better one, don't knock mine," Norma King said tartly.

Waving to a co-worker who was also leaving the building, he threaded quickly between cars idling at the red light, headed for the parking across the street, and made it safely to the other side. "Mom, I'm concerned about a stranger looking after the kids and staying in my house."

"Adam, anybody other than me will be a stranger until you get to know them. At least the girl is related to someone I know."

"As if that makes it better," he muttered. He stopped and looked around the huge parking lot that Family Care shared with two other businesses, his mother's 'I heard that' response vague noise as his eyes scanned cars. Now where had Steve parked his vehicle? Earlier they'd done a home visit together and had used Adam's mini-van. Steve had dropped him in front of the office before parking, so he didn't know where on this huge lot the van was. He clicked the remote access a few times. Nothing. It hadn't been working properly for some time now. He'd have to call him.

"Will seven o'clock this evening work?" his mother asked him.

He sighed. This was inevitable. His mother had helped him for five years with the kids, postponing her retirement. Now she had to go to Florida. His stepfather had been there too long alone, and his complaints had gotten very vocal of late. "I suppose so," he agreed, sounding like he was about to deplane without a parachute.

"Be a little more enthusiastic. You don't want to chase her out the door before she even enters."

That was going to take effort, he thought. Aloud he said, "I'll try. Talk to you later mom." *Lord, Cheyenne, why did you have to die?* He killed that thought. If he let it linger, he would break down in this parking lot, and make a fool of himself bawling in public. Adam wished he could block the pain of losing her the way he blocked his thoughts. He dialed Steve.

***

Jasmine drove with care, her speedometer way below the forty miles per hour speed limit. She'd already speared three deer with her headlights. She didn't intend to spear any with her car, although the car might very likely sustain more damage than the deer. They were such unpredictable creatures.

Forest Hill Road was what she was searching for. With the towering pines that seemed to grow in stature the deeper into Mohawk Valley she drove, Adam King's road was appropriately named. Jasmine felt a little nervous, the way she always did before an interview. What would he ask her? She had been a teacher for twelve of her thirty-four years. She loved children, which was why she taught elementary. She could help form characters for time and eternity. It gave her satisfaction, made her feel like she was making a difference, even though it would never be for her own child. Jasmine blinked, removing the thought with a single eye movement. She needed this job and dwelling on that errant thought would make her too depressed to convince a potential employer that she was emotionally stable enough to care for kids.

The next sign ended her search. Jasmine made the turn and looked for number fourteen. The houses were set too far back from the road for her to see numbers on doors; so she settled for reading the digits on mailboxes. Six houses down, she made another right. The Ford Focus's tires crunched over dirt and gravel; and then, with a little bump, the ride smoothed out as tires found blacktop. Jasmine rolled to a halt before an expansive white house with black shutters. Two Roman-like columns flagged the front doors, towering above the three semi-circular steps leading to the front entrance.

She killed the engine and whispered a prayer that all would go well. When she left here tonight, she planned to leave in possession of a job. Public school teaching jobs for the new school year set to start in fifteen days were all gone. Her only hope had been the position pulled from beneath her yesterday with the Indian Run SAB

School. She planned to apply for substitute teaching with the district. Thank God she'd maintained her New York State teaching license even though she had moved to Florida right after she initially got it. With this job though, she might not need it. Still, Jasmine liked to keep her options open, although subbing might not even be an option. With the recession still running, there were far more teachers than jobs available in the field. How depressing. Jesus really needs to come, she thought as she exited her vehicle. You know times were bad when it took humongous effort for the educated to get employed. More sellers than buyers—a popular saying. In this case it was more job-seekers than jobs. She rang the bell.

***

Adam had been expecting somebody more mature, somebody more capable of managing children. But this tiny woman looked hardly older than a teenager, and if she topped the twins by an inch it would be a miracle. Could she handle his kids? Not that they were difficult, but sometimes you needed width and weight to enforce rules.

He must have been staring too long in consternation, because her cheerful smile started fading. Adam pulled himself together and played the part of interviewer setting interviewee at ease. "Ms. Lewis," he greeted formally, extending his hand. "It's nice to meet you."

Jasmine had the feeling a great deal of disconnect existed between what he said and how he felt. Adam King didn't think it was nice to meet her at all. His lengthy stare of dismay had communicated that loud and clear. But since he didn't have the whole acting thing cornered, she strut her skills too. Infusing her smile with effulgence once more—she'd been told this thing she did with her mouth was incredible—she accepted his handshake and said it was nice to meet him.

That formality finished, Jasmine accepted his invitation to step inside. Hardwood, honey colored and polished to mirror shine; white walls; and a teardrop chandelier hanging from the ceiling and twirling gently made the foyer beautiful and showcase-like. The family portraits on the walls made it warm and homey.

Jasmine moved closer to look at the first picture. It framed four children in school uniforms, smiling into the camera: Two boys and two girls. "Adam, Jr., Drew, Claire, and Dona." She touched each face as she called their names.

"How did you know?" he asked surprised.

"I'm a teacher. I'm around kids a lot, and I know who looks what age. My mother told me their names and ages. The rest was a piece of cake." She looked around. "Speaking of mothers, where's Norma? I thought she would be here too."

He thought his mother would have been here as well. "A friend came and took her to a surprise party for another friend. What she doesn't know is that the party's hers—a farewell—and she's the one who's going to be surprised."

"That sounds like fun," Jasmine laughed.

"I'm sure it will be for her, but I'm sorry to see her go, which is why you are here."

Was that grimace an attempt at a smile? Jasmine started having second thoughts about this job. She didn't want to deal with a hostile employer every day. Well maybe not hostile but one who wished she were someone else, like his mother.

"Shall we?" He pushed the heavy cherry door on the left wall inwards and motioned her ahead of him.

Jasmine stepped into a study well illuminated by fluorescent lights. Bookshelves lined every wall except the one housing the window. A stalwart oak desk occupied most of the center of a room that was more long than wide. A MacBook Air rested atop the desk along with several sheets of typewritten papers. Two stacks of books sat off to the right side, their arrangement atop each other haphazard and just waiting for catastrophe's catalyst—a swung arm or body brush—to strike. Her mother told her he was a preacher. Maybe he'd been preparing his Sabbath sermon.

"Have a seat, please." He gestured to the left where three armchairs, tan, ivory, and tan surrounded a coffee table.

Jasmine moved forward and took the chair on the left. He sat across from her. Even with him seated, she had to look up. How tall was he? Six four, six five? She watched him sit back and cross his knee as if in preparation for an interrogation. And with his expression still struggling to strike a balance between somberness and pleasantness, Jasmine felt like this interview would be an interrogation. His jaw line looked hard and resistant to change. A smile didn't stand a chance of relaxing it. His strong chin solidified the picture. And his full mouth was set in solemn lines that looked permanent. Overall he had a firm and solid face—very much like his body. While on the lean side, his physique came from fitness. She could tell from the play of muscles across his back that the neat-fitting dress shirt didn't hide when he moved. In the brief moment she had stood behind him while he opened the study's door, Jasmine had admired that view as well as the narrowness of his waist and hips. He had an easy, confident walk, each step taken as if he owned the world and had all the time to traverse it with the power of those long legs. From face to physique he carried a compelling air, a brooding kind of magnetism that drew a woman's attention. Jasmine realized Adam King had drawn hers. Startled, she looked away.

CHAPTER II

Adam knew he couldn't ask her age. However, her youthful looks bothered him. How old was she exactly? Just because she was a teacher didn't pre-qualify her for the job he was offering. She wasn't married and didn't have children of her own. His mom mentioned that. Qualifications for motherhood came from internship. You learned from experience only, by being a mother to a child. In that sunflower yellow sundress with what appeared to be Bumble bees flying around the hem, she looked like she needed a mother herself.

His eyes slid over her face, assessing. Her butterscotch complexion had to be a product of her mixed ancestry, which appeared to be a blend of African-American and Asian. Tiny eyes, coal colored, elongated ovals met and held his stare for some beats before moving to some point beyond him. Her small, upturned nose seemed to tip up a bit more as if in defiance, although he didn't know to what. That action made her glasses slide backwards down a nearly non-existent bridge. The thin titanium frame held lens as small and compact as the person wearing them. In fact everything about her was concise and neat from the crown of her head, with every strand of hair smoothed back into a bun, to her chin. Well, there was one aberration from the norm...her mouth: Full and wide, the fringes of her lips appeared to be crafted by the tip of a gifted artist's pen—its upper edges forming the cursive letter 'm' and looking like gently formed peaks with sloping sides.

"Ahem," Adam cleared his throat, feeling warm and uncomfortable all of a sudden. "How long have you been teaching, Ms. Lewis?"

Hadn't he gotten the resume that she emailed? Maybe he was warming up to the relevant questions. "Twelve years," she answered him.

"Are you taking a Sabbatical from teaching this year?"

Jasmine had anticipated the question. She briefly explained what happened with the job she'd returned to New York for.

"So this position is a temporary, stepping stone opportunity for you," he said, frowning.

It was, but it sounded bad when put like that. "If hired, my commitment would be good through the school year."

"But afterwards, you would go back to teaching?"

"Yes," Jasmine answered honestly. She didn't see the point in lying. If it cost her the job, so be it. He frowned some more. His gaze flickered briefly to his phone's screen, and then he looked up. "I see that you taught the first, fourth and sixth grades during your teaching career."

It was an observation. Jasmine didn't reply.

"You don't appear to have any experience dealing with teenagers. I have two."

His statement came out skeptical, and Jasmine took it as criticism. She felt a kick of resistance in her belly but controlled it. "This is a profession-specific resume, Pastor King. That means it's unique to teaching. If I'd had time I would have adjusted it to be more comprehensive and reflective of *all* my experiences as they relate to dealing with children." She smiled but knew from the way his right eyebrow edged towards his hairline, he'd heard the patronage that she hadn't fought too hard to camouflage. A bit of rebellion had reached the surface. Her sweet smile didn't say 'sorry,' and she did not speak that word.

"Well, Ms. Lewis," he glanced at his watch, "we have a little time now, so why don't you *enlighten* me as to how comprehensive that experience is?"

Watch it! He's a potential employer. No tit for tat here. Control your tongue. She widened her smile, took a breath, and took a shot at obedience. "I've been a Sabbath School teacher for about four years at my church in Florida. I taught the junior and early-teenage class as well as the teenagers, fourteen to eighteen. I've also acted as chaperone for several youth trips. So, you see, I do have experience supervising and teaching this group."

He made a steeple with his fingers and touched them to the tip of his chin, his expression turning thoughtful. "Teaching young people for an hour or two on Sabbath or chaperoning them overnight or even for a weekend is different from providing care and guidance for them every day, Ms. Lewis. That's what you'll be doing—giving everyday care—if you acquire this position."

Had she imagined it or had he stressed the 'if'?

"Let me tell you a bit about the job and my expectations, and then you can have a better idea if your skill sets are up to it."

Jasmine felt her hackles rise. *If* she was up to it! The man didn't know squat about her except for the lines of her credentials in that email. He thought her incapable of babysitting four children? Unless, he knew something that she didn't, she was overqualified for the job. "Pastor King, do your children have learning or behavioral problems that I should be aware of?"

He looked affronted. "No."

The kids weren't the problem; he was. Jasmine straightened in her seat and looked him dead in the eye. "That means I don't need a special education certification to deal with them. Why then am I getting the sense that you don't want to hire me?"

Both his eyebrows rose at her direct approach. Once more his gaze swept her from top to toe.

Why does he keep doing that? Jasmine wondered. His next words explained it.

"Okay, since you were frank, I'll return the favor. I have rules in my house which I expect to be obeyed. I'm not always here to ensure that they are adhered to. My mother has been a blessing in these five years since my wife died, but the kids get away with a lot in terms of their household responsibilities. She's sweet; she's their grandmother, so she allows it. She thinks I'm too hard on them. If children are to grow up to be responsible and productive citizens, they must have order in their lives and discipline. That means they need to consistently do what they are assigned and understand that there are consequences. If necessary, those consequences need to be enforced."

His eyes did that visual sweep again.

"Now, Ms. Lewis, I may be stepping on eggshells here, but I have to say it. You don't look old enough or big enough to manage yourself much less four children. I'm not sure you can maintain order in my house."

Jasmine was stunned. He doubted her ability because of her size and age, which he didn't even know? This was a first. Being Jasmine, quick-tongued and feisty, she answered him with spirit, "What century is this again? Since when did bulk rather than brain start influencing a woman's ability to do a job?"

"You are making this into a sexist concern. I can assure you that it's not."

His calm in the face of her disquiet made Jasmine more agitated. She was small. So what? She had no control over her size or youthful look. Her body bulk or lack of it didn't make her inadequate or incapable. That single thought shifted her annoyance with Adam King to dislike of him. One other man had accused her of inadequacy because of her size. She'd endured it for three years, thinking he was right, thinking she could find a way to please him. She'd actually considered changing her tiny endowments into titanic ones just to keep a worthless man. Thank God, she had woken up in time. Otherwise now she would have had implants and a myriad of medical issues while he was off with a woman who could give him what he wanted—a voluptuous body and a baby.

She hadn't taught Simon a lesson—her one regret. But this oversized buffoon sitting across from her was going to eat his words and his thought that she was inadequate. When she finished with him, he would eat humble pie and have a new vocabulary that did not include inadequate. To do that, though, she needed to get this job.

Jasmine brushed imaginary lint from the sleeve of her black jacket. She sat back in the chair and crossed her ankles. Not one trace of her inner anger was visible. She was the picture of poise and serenity. She asked him, "Weren't you going to tell me about the job requirements?"

His eyebrows dipped towards his nostrils as her unexpected action seemed to confuse him. But he answered her. "I'll need a sitter or chaperone, if you prefer, from Monday to Friday. The older kids need to be up by six o'clock to catch the school bus which passes by at six-fifty. Adam is good with timeliness but Claire isn't.

She has braids in yet she spends time doodling with styles every morning. Drew and Dona are in grade five. Their bus comes at nine, so they don't have to get up until around seven-thirty."

"Does the bus stop at this address?"

"Yes, out here, it stops at each home."

She supposed there were perks for paying hefty taxes in suburbia. When she taught in New York City, the buses stopped at designated areas and the kids had to walk sometimes a long block to get picked up. "What time do they get home?"

"Claire and Adam get here at two-thirty and Drew and Dona by three-fifty."

"What about their diet? What do they eat?" She hoped they were vegetarians. She was vegan, and it had been years since she had prepared fish or chicken.

"We're not vegans. We use eggs."

Which meant they were vegetarians? She asked to be sure. "So that means you're vegetarians, right?"

"Right. As to what they eat, they love bread—too much if you ask me. My mother used to bake, but even if you do, it's not a requirement."

She didn't bake—at least not bread—but she didn't tell him so. He'd already started talking again anyway.

"Regarding meal preparation, whenever my mom had to be away, which wasn't too often, I kept it simple. Pasta is my friend because it's easy to prepare. I know how to make a good sauce. We make use of the vegetarian meat alternatives. The fridge is always stocked. They do take lunches to school, so you'll have to prepare those. They'll need breakfast and dinner when they come home. So basically you'd be responsible for three meals a day. The hours between nine and two-thirty are yours to spend how you wish. The younger kids will need help with homework. By seven o'clock everything should be done. Everybody should be in bed by nine o'clock. Your weekends are your own. If you're here, it's as if you're not here. We won't bother you—that is if you choose to board with us. My mom says she mentioned the compensation. I'm not sure which way you would want to go."

So he was going to give her the job. Mostly because she wanted to set him on his ear, she said, "Why don't I meet the kids first and then decide the direction." Sending him a cheerful smile, she added,

"Maybe I won't need to take a direction at all."

His face changed. His expression, which had grown more relaxed as he spoke, turned cool and withdrawn. Goodness, he was so anal. Didn't he ever joke? She sighed. "When can I meet the kids?"

"Right now if you want to."

"I do."

He texted something on his phone. Less than a minute later footsteps pounded upstairs and then what sounded like a stampede descended the stairs. Jasmine expected the study's door to burst open and a bunch of exuberant, sweating children to tumble inside. Instead a soft knock sounded on the door. At Adam King's command to 'enter,' the door swung inwards slowly and a tall boy, Adam Jr., walked in followed by his siblings. He had the same oak brown complexion of his father. The long nose, full mouth, and strong jaw line were the same, but his features didn't have the hard and unyielding quality that time and something else had stamped into his father's face. The girl with the braids and hazelnut complexion was Claire. She gave a hesitant smile, glancing from her dad to Jasmine, flashing silver braces over her teeth. Dona and Drew had a strong resemblance despite being fraternal. They didn't resemble their father, so Jasmine assumed they favored their mom. Dona was smiling, but Drew looked like he'd rather be elsewhere.

"Kids, come and meet Jasmine Lewis. If all goes well, she'll be taking over from grandma."

Jasmine stood as the children approached. Adam set the example for his siblings to follow. He extended his hand. "Nice to meet you, Miss. Lewis," he said. The shake was firm and quick, just like his smile, which she noticed didn't reach his eyes. Claire came next. She gave a quick shake and a shy smile. If it weren't for her and Dona, Jasmine would think that smiling in this family was taboo.

Introductions over, awkwardness set in as the kids kept standing there, obviously unsure of how to proceed. Jasmine took conversational initiative. "I noticed a picture of you guys in uniforms in the hall." She gestured to the right. "Which school do you attend?"

"That picture's two years old. We go to public school now," Adam explained.

"That would be the Mohawk Valley School district, right?"

He nodded.

"What's the name of your school?"

"Mohawk Valley High." The duh-uh was faint, but it was there. Jasmine ignored it.

She turned to Claire. "How do you like the school? I hear you and Adam attend the same one."

The girl's shy smile skittered across her mouth as she answered, her voice mouse-like low. "It's okay. It's really big though."

"I bet there's a lot of walking involved," Jasmine observed, trying to draw her out and relax her. She noticed the fingers Claire wrapped around her arm were cutting off her circulation, and the child didn't seem to notice. Jasmine didn't know if she was nervous conversing or if it was a natural state for her.

"A lot." The exhalation that followed the admission conveyed the magnitude of the daily distance covered.

Jasmine grinned. "When I was in college, I think I lost fifteen pounds the first month, walking back and forth across campus to my classes."

"Well all the walking is in this one humongous building!" the girl complained, releasing the grip on her arm and placing her hands on her hips in frustration.

Jasmine smiled both at her expression of aggravation as well as the evidence that she was relaxing and participating in this conversation. "On the bright side, you'll burn all your daily calories even without gym."

"I think that they should exempt us from it." Her smile this time was full and mischievous.

"Wishful thinking," Jasmine said, feeling pleased that she'd pulled Claire out of her shell. "Maybe you can do without it. You're fit. Nice blouse by the way." The pink blouse got its style and statement from the sequined musical notes strewn across a scale set diagonally across the blouse's front.

Claire smiled very big. "Thanks," she said, her eyes sparkling at the simple compliment, making Jasmine wonder if she got them much.

"And which school do you go to?" She directed the question at Dona.

"Morgan Wendell Middle School," she blurted as if she'd been waiting with bated breath to be addressed.

"And what's it like?"

"It's great. I love my teacher and I've got lots of friends. I love my school."

"What about you, Drew?" Jasmine sent him an encouraging smile, hoping to coax a return smile and an answer out of the seemingly quiet boy. "Do you like your school?"

He shrugged. "It's okay."

Jasmine wasn't sure how to respond to that flat, disinterested answer; so she said in an upbeat voice, "Well let's just hope it will be good by the first day of school."

"Alright kids. Go back upstairs and finish your homework," Adam spoke up.

"I'm done with my homework," Drew told him.

"Have you read yet?" His father looked at him with suspicion.

"Not yet," he muttered.

"Then read a chapter while I finish talking with Ms. Lewis."

Jasmine stopped their departure with an outstretched arm. "Wait. Do you have any questions for me?" She looked at each child, meeting their eyes, and smiling in encouragement, wanting them to feel comfortable and confident talking to her.

"I have a question," Drew said, surprising her.

She turned to him expectantly.

"How old are you?"

"Drew!" The reproof didn't come from his dad. Claire was the one who spoke.

"What?" Drew asked, his tone suggesting that his sister was making a big deal for nothing. "She looks like a kid."

"It's all right," Jasmine soothed Claire's concern. While surprised by Drew's question, she felt glad that he'd voiced what he was thinking. It showed her that he was an observer, a quiet person who noticed things like her youthful appearance and wondered about it. "That's a good question," she said to Drew. "I'm thirty-four."

"Wow, you look like Claire's sister," the boy said, looking at her face and figure in wonder.

"Oh, you are so sweet," Jasmine beamed at him. "You've made my day." Glancing at Claire, she said, "I hope you don't mind that he thinks we look like sisters."

The girl shook her head. "I don't mind. It'll be fun when we go shopping. We're the same size."

Jasmine laughed and said in a stage whisper. "I'm a two. What are you?"

"I'm zero," Claire whispered back.

"We're practically equal. Shopping will be a blast!" Both of them started laughing and even the boys began chuckling when Dona put in, "I'm your size too. Can I shop with you?"

Adam watched the exchange from his vantage point in the chair, feeling a bit like an outsider in the exchange. She was good—very good with kids. She knew how to connect and knew how to do it fast. Since Cheyenne died, the kids tended not to get too attached to people. One psychologist said it was the fear of loss from their mother's death that still lingered. They were afraid to get close to somebody in case the person died. Yet in a single conversation Jasmine Lewis had breached their reserve. She'd piqued Drew's curiosity and gotten him to talk to her. That was a first. Drew didn't talk much and to strangers not at all. Truth be told, Drew hardly spoke to him or his grandmother.

While he still had his reservations about her ability to enforce the rules in this house, Adam knew he would hire Jasmine Lewis. The kids accepted her and that was key. Whether she knew it or not and very likely she did, the children liking her would make it easier for her to care for them. In the final analysis, this was about them and their needs. It mattered little that there were things about Jasmine Lewis that bothered him. This wasn't about him or the fact that the bubbly sound of her laughter made flutters feather through his insides; or that the parting of her lips into that incredible smile made his breath hitch somewhere between his chest and throat; or even that her shapely ankles crossed over each other made him heady thinking about another finely formed and curvaceous part of her just below her collar bones. Like everything on her neat, compact frame, those two beautiful evidences of her gender were just right in size and shape.

Adam cleared his throat, more to clear his thoughts than to get the attention of the others in the room. Now every eye turned his way. His eyes flickered to Jasmine and then away. He felt like a culprit and as if she might disapprove if she read his thoughts. She was a pretty, youthful-looking woman. It was hard for a man not to notice that. Adam gritted his teeth. This was not the time for his hibernating libido to surface. Before craving crushed good sense, he spoke, "Kids, why don't you go back upstairs? Ms. Lewis and I need to talk."

They left, closing the door behind them.

As the door clicked shut, Jasmine took her time turning around to face Adam King. She followed that action with a plastic smile. Looking up at the man towering head and shoulders over her, she said, "So, Pastor King, what's the verdict? Am I hired or not?"

CHAPTER III

Return to her hometown had never been in either Scarlet Norman's long term or short term life plans. But life had a way of throwing you curve balls, and you ended up doing things that were never on your radar. So here she was, back in Mohawk Valley, going on two years now. Globalization had collateral damage, and she had been hit twice. Scarlet opted out of a third victimization. She had been a marketing executive for two pharmaceutical companies. After they launched worldwide operations, her job had twice become obsolete. They didn't need her anymore. That's when she'd heard about web copywriting and found a perfect marriage between her pharmaceutical industry knowledge and writing sales copy for websites for industry businesses.

During transition between professions, she returned to her childhood home in Mohawk Valley. The property belonged to her and her siblings—a house which none of them had wanted but couldn't sell as per their deceased parents' will. Her stay would have been temporary, but a local minister who just happened to be single caught her very single and searching eye. A copywriter wasn't desk or location bound. She could live and write from anywhere and still make a living. Mohawk Valley became home again. The Mt. Calvary SAB Church became her house of worship. Pastor Adam King became the man she planned to marry.

The very slight problem was that Pastor Adam King wasn't interested in marrying ever again. They had gotten close enough for him to once share the tragedy of his wife's death and how he didn't think he would ever recover from that devastation to consider courting much less marrying another woman. Flirtation and use of womanly wiles wouldn't work with him then. Scarlet decided to chase him from another angle. She had brokered many marketing deals over the years and secured difficult and impossible to acquire accounts. Capturing Pastor King's heart became a challenging account that she was determined to acquire. To that end, she had worked her way into church positions that placed her in close working contact with the pastor, positions which showcased her competence and dependability and which had made her his *go to* girl, so to speak. She currently served as church clerk, risk manager, and assistant to the First Elder. She was shooting for the First Eldership next year.

She turned in the minutes of every meeting in record time; made sure the church's insurance stayed current; and ensured that the building stayed within town codes for the recent building expansion, and that any safety hazards like broken steps or shaky railings were corrected on discovery. She never refused a task when called upon by the pastor to perform it. She was the only elder who consistently agreed to conduct prayer meeting if the pastor could not do it. She served with him every Sabbath. She made sure she knew every member by name and got acquainted with every visitor. If somebody was missing, she let the pastor know. If somebody returned to church after being missing a week or two, she slipped him a note during service, so that he could acknowledge that person. She made herself valuable. He appreciated her service and professionalism. He told her so. She hoped that pretty soon he'd appreciate her as a woman.

***

After two weeks on the job, Jasmine decided that motherhood involved much more than meets the eye. And she wasn't even mother, just the babysitter. She started three weeks after the interview and on the first day of school. On the first day of her second week at work, everything ran smoothly until Claire called, sounding frantic, and said the school bus was coming and she'd left her gym clothes. She didn't want to get detention. Could Jasmine bring them please? The clothes weren't in the girl's room. It was a good thing Norma showed her the clean folded laundry she'd left in the basement, arranged according to owners.

Riffling fast through the pile that she hoped was Claire's and not Dona's—they were close in size anyway—Jasmine grabbed a pair of shorts and a t-shirt and ran back upstairs. Nearly out the door, she remembered in the nick of time that it was a long way to the road. Grabbing her keys, she jumped in her car and sped down the driveway only to see the taillights of the bus disappearing down the road.

She hadn't gone through all that breathlessness for nothing. She raced after it like the NYPD chasing a suspect, tooting her horn the whole way. The driver pulled over either because of the racket she was making or to pick up another child. Jasmine was just glad that he'd stopped. She swung around the bus and stopped in front of it. Claire came to the door and took her clothes with a grateful smile. That evening they had both laughed about the chase.

Drew left his lunch that same day. She took it to school for him only to find it uneaten in his lunch box that evening. Why hadn't he eaten it after she'd gone through the trouble to bring it? He didn't like that particular meat-alternative. In the classroom, it had been one lesson plan for thirty kids. In the homeroom, one size didn't fit all or in this case one meal didn't match all. She reworked his lunch the next time.

Over the course of the week, she'd learned their likes and dislikes in the food department. She'd also found that they pushed the limit when it came to the bedtime hour. Adam in particular resisted the curfew. Oh, he didn't do it overtly by refusing to go to bed. He went to bed alright, but he wasn't sleeping. After listening at the boys' bedroom door for three nights, Jasmine realized he was on the phone up to eleven o'clock one night. She spoke to him about it two consecutive times. On the third night, she entered the room without knocking and took the phone from him. He'd been very vocal in his displeasure with that and demanded his phone back. Jasmine told him she'd return it in the morning and closed the door. Now he wasn't speaking to her. No sweat. Teenagers sulked a lot when they didn't get their way. He'd get over it.

***

Apparently he didn't. At nine o'clock the following night, Adam asked her to meet him in his study. Jasmine wondered what he wanted. She hadn't seen him all week except for brief moments in the morning when he was rushing out the door, or in the evening when he came in, and just before he locked himself in his study. Jasmine knew he was a busy man. He not only worked as a pastor but as a counselor too. He also had an adjunct professorship with the local community college. He taught psychology two mornings a week at Mohawk Community College. Despite all this, Jasmine felt that he needed to make time for his kids. She didn't observe any interaction between them. She understood that he was the sole breadwinner in the home and he had to work to make ends meet, but children needed their parents. Once during the week, Claire had stated that she wished her dad didn't have to work so hard and that she could see more of him.

Jasmine silently pledged that she'd find a way to speak to Adam King about setting aside more time in his schedule for his kids. If she'd had any to call her own, she would spend every moment she could with them. Jasmine believed that children were a blessing from God, even more so to her, because she would never have one to call her own.

She knocked on the door of the study and entered. Adam looked up from his Mac.

"Ms. Lewis." He nodded a greeting and pointed to the chair beside the desk. "Please, have a seat."

Jasmine sat down and studied him. He looked exhausted. His eyes were weary and red as if he'd been looking at a computer screen for too long. He pressed his fingers to his eyelids briefly and scrubbed a hand down his face, unwittingly confirming her thoughts about his tiredness. Jasmine's heart shifted with concern. "Would you like a cup of tea?" she asked, thinking that a cup of chamomile might help him to relax.

He glanced at her, startled at the unexpected inquiry. "No, thanks. I want to talk to you about Adam."

Jasmine's spine stiffened. She knew where this wind was blowing. "What about him?" she asked calmly.

He sat back in his office chair and folded his arms across his chest. "He told me that you confiscated his phone last night."

"Did he tell you why?" Jasmine raised her eyebrows, the question flavored a bit with spunk.

"He was on it after curfew, but th—"

"For the third night in a row," she interrupted, emphasizing the magnitude of the misdeed.

"Yes, I know all that, but that's not the part I have a problem with."

"Oh?" There were parts to this now? And why would he have a problem? Hadn't he been concerned about her maintaining order in his household? Now he had a problem when she fulfilled his wishes?

"When Adam got his phone back there were three international calls made from it. Two to Jamaica and one to St. Thomas."

Jasmine sat statue-still in her chair, hearing the accusation he hadn't articulated. She raised a forefinger, "Wait one minute. If there were international calls on his phone, I didn't make them."

"The times of the calls were when you had the phone in your possession," he pointed out.

He still hadn't accused her outright, but he didn't have to. He believed she made those calls. That was clearer than day. Adam King, Jr. was a crafty boy. She hadn't expected this. Jasmine wouldn't underestimate him again, but if he thought he could intimidate her into not enforcing the rules his dad put in place, he'd better think twice. But first things first. One problem at a time. "Look, Pastor King, I just told you I did not make those calls. Obviously you don't believe me. The fact that you've persisted with the issue by pointing out that I had the phone at the times of the calls, implying that no other person could have made the calls, tells me that you'll believe your son's word over mine. I understand that. I'm a stranger still, and he's your child. However, you might want to consider a couple of things: I have my own phone. Why would I use your son's? The day we met, you doubted whether I understood teenagers or whether I could care for them. At the risk of being insubordinate, I'm now wondering how much *you* understand teenagers?"

He leaned forward in his chair, his expression hard. The chill in his eyes said her words had struck a chord. Jasmine wasn't trying to get fired, but she'd learned it's best to start as you mean to go on. Don't take things docilely, especially when you're not at fault. Be firm, frank, and as much as possible be polite, but speak your mind.

"Have you considered that Adam was the one who made those calls?" she asked.

"Why would he do that?" His tone could turn a water droplet to an icicle.

"Because he was angry that I took his phone, he wanted to get back at me. He probably hoped to intimidate me into not doing it again if he got me in trouble with you."

"You don't know my children like I do, Ms. Lewis. Adam isn't the kind of child to be cunning like that," he objected.

"Sometimes I wonder if you know your children at all, Pastor." Okay she was having a problem with the 'be polite' part. Now the words were out, and she could not take them back. Jasmine didn't try to fix it because she couldn't.

"What's that supposed to mean?" His eyebrows went south and his mouth firmed into a displeased line, annoyance shadowing his expression like storm clouds darkening the skies.

"You work all the time. They don't see you. Do you know that Claire wishes you worked fewer hours so you could spend more time with her? Do you know that Adam sleeps restlessly some nights and cries out for you?" She watched surprise and hurt do a fast exchange in his expression before he camouflaged it. "And do you know that he also cries out for his mother?"

"Enough!" The word struck like thunder, cracking the air like lightning.

Jasmine jerked and watched pain and anger perform a visible struggle in his face. He inhaled a significant portion of the oxygen in the air and exhaled slowly. "I might not know everything there is to know about my kids," he started, his voice tight and his words measured. "And maybe I do need to spend time with them," he continued through his teeth. "But you don't know them period. You don't know any of us. You have no idea what we've been through as a family, what we still go through. Do me a favor and clear it with me before you punish my kids and please don't ever mention their mother again. Goodnight, Ms. Lewis." With that he left his chair and opened the door.

Stunned, she sat there for some moments before grasping that this was a dismissal. She rose slowly and approached the door with even more lethargic steps. At the door she paused, not sure what to say, but feeling compelled to make an exit statement. She looked up at him, but he was staring determinedly at some point beyond her, his jaw like granite. Jasmine wet her lips. "I'm sorry. I didn't mean to stir up old hurts. I was just trying to—"

"Good. Night. Ms. Lewis." The words came out with forceful pace, the emotion in them bordering on violence.

Jasmine sailed out the door. She knew when she had overstayed her welcome.

***

An hour later, Jasmine glanced up from her devotional at the soft knock on her door. She was still dressed in her jeans and a T-shirt; so she said, "Come in."

Adam, Jr.'s head popped in.

Jasmine was surprised. She thought he was in bed.

"May I talk to you?" he asked.

"Sure."

He came in and left the door slightly open. He paced half way across the room and put his hands into the pockets of his lounge pants. The way his gaze kept shifting from her to various places in the room and the way he kept biting his lips cued her in that he had something difficult to say.

"What is it, Adam?" She gave him an opening.

He blew out a weighty breath. "I'm sorry for what I did."

Jasmine raised a brow. What was he apologizing for?

"I'm the one who made those international calls and told dad that you did it. I wanted to get you in trouble because I was mad that you'd taken my phone. It was wrong and I'm sorry."

"Well it's very mature of you to admit it and to apologize."

"It's not maturity. Dad made me do it, and he took my phone away for a day."

Adam believed her? He hadn't acted as if he had. His son's apology proved it though. "Thanks for apologizing," she told the boy.

"Thanks for accepting. Good night." He turned and left the room.

Jasmine picked up the devotional but didn't read it. She wondered what had brought Adam's about face.

***

In his study, Adam looked at the picture he'd put away for over a year: Cheyenne. Storing it in the drawer of his desk hadn't erased the pain as he'd hoped; it had just eased it a little. Tonight that feisty Jasmine Lewis had stirred up his agony. Why did she have to

29

mention that Adam yearned for his mother in his dreams? To hear that his kids hurt from Cheyenne's absence hurt him too and resurrected the pain of her passing.

He trailed his fingers across her cheek, admired her mocha brown skin, her carefree smile and imagined laughter tumbling from her lips...just like it had on the day she died. He closed his eyes against a memory that suddenly wouldn't go away. They'd been on vacation in Florida. They'd taken the kids to The Magic Kingdom and Universal Studios in Orlando. Later they went further south to enjoy the beaches. It was the day before they returned home. Cheyenne and the kids wanted to hit the beach one last time. Wiped out from all the places they had visited, he hadn't wanted to go, but he'd gone because they'd insisted. There wasn't a day he didn't wish he'd made a different choice, had stuck to his guns, insisted that they rest. If he had...

Adam closed his eyes. The shouts from swimmers in the ocean echoed in his ears. He saw the lifeguards rushing in and bringing out someone who'd had a heart attack in the water. The crowd swelled fast, the chatter and noise even faster as word spread along the shore about what had happened. Soon the ambulance's sirens added to the crescendo of sound. He looked around then and didn't see Cheyenne. The kids had been nearby building a sandcastle when the commotion occurred. Worried he scanned the crowd to no avail. Just when he looked towards the ocean another shout went up and the lifeguards started running. Shouting to Adam to stay put and watch the kids, he ran after the guards, fearing what he would find, hoping he was wrong, praying that the body they were towing in wasn't Cheyenne...but the prayer had been for nothing.

***

Jasmine balanced the tray on an upraised knee and opened the study's door after knocking once. Two steps in, she froze. Adam King had his head in his hands and from his tortured and repetitive whispers of *Why God? Why?*, she figured her timing was atrocious. She shouldn't have followed her tendency to help everybody and their dog by fixing him the cup of tea he'd refused earlier and adding to the offering a sandwich and fruit. Now if she could just ease out the way she'd come, he would be none the wiser. Just one more step backwards and his privacy would be preserved.

Jasmine didn't know how it happened. Since the devil was a convenient scapegoat, she blamed it on him later. With her final step half executed, the tray slipped, spilling hot tea on her thigh. Jasmine dropped the tray and jumped halfway to the ceiling as agony shot through her leg like an inferno. "Ouuuuuch!" She exclaimed, both hands grabbing for her burning thigh.

Before she could draw another breath, her feet left the floor and she cruised through air. Walls rushed by as Adam King flew through the foyer to the kitchen, his hard chest a cushion against her side and his strong arms surrounding her like a fortress.

"Unzip your Jeans," he commanded, seating her on the granite counter top of the island in the kitchen.

Jasmine stared at him dumbly, the fire in her thigh dulling a little at his scandalous suggestion. She watched him saturate a pantry towel beneath the tap at the kitchen's sink and turn to her. He made an impatient sound when he saw she hadn't obeyed him. He scooped her off the counter and had his hand on her zipper before her protest flew out.

"What are you doing?" she squeaked in alarm, slapping at his hand to stop him. She sucked in a long sharp breath when he pulled down the Jeans and they rubbed against her burning skin. Crossing her hands before her, trying to preserve her modesty, her breath rushed out when he slapped the cold pantry towel on her thigh, covering the red skin that was already puckering into a blister.

Outraged modesty or not, the cold compress cooled the burn instantly.

She wanted to say thanks but couldn't find her words. It wasn't embarrassment alone, but he was kneeling before her, one hand holding the compress against her thigh, his line of sight pelvic low while her only protection there was Joe Boxer briefs for girls. The one good thing was that he appeared oblivious to her state of undress. His only focus, his full concern seemed to be her injured thigh, nothing higher or lower.

He changed the compress, switching one soothing towel for another. "Better?" he asked after holding it there for a while.

She nodded.

"Think you can make it to your room?"

Another nod confirmed that she could.

"You'll need to change this every five minutes or so for the next hour. If it gets unbearable or if you think you need to go to the emergency room, let me know."

She didn't have health insurance, so the emergency department was out of the question. She didn't think it warranted a hospital visit though. "It feels better, thanks."

"Okay, hold this against it."

Their fingers brushed as he withdrew and she placed her hand where his had been. A funny little tingle skipped across her finger tips. Jasmine bit her lip and looked at the floor. She found the man aggravating most of the time, but that bit of electricity wasn't irritation. What was it then?

"Here take this."

She glanced up to find him unbuttoning his shirt.

What was he doing?

"Your Jeans will irritate the burn if you pull them up. Wear my shirt in case you meet the kids coming down for water or something."

The sight of his well built arms and shoulders fried the agreement on the tip of her tongue. Toned muscles shifted as Adam freed himself from the sleeves of his shirt. Saliva drifted down Jasmine's throat. His close-fitting undershirt provided no barrier between her eyes and her imagination, and she conjured every muscle as her gaze slid down his chest, following the flow of the undershirt over his toned abs.

"Put your arm through."

Jasmine blinked and jerked her eyes guiltily away from ogling his chest. Had he noticed? She hoped not. Automatically, she thrust her right arm into the shirt sleeve he held. He took the cold cloth from her so she could put her other arm in. The elbows trailed nearly to her wrists and the shirt's tails fell to her knees, but the garment restored her modesty. Jasmine added thoughtful and tender to her list of descriptors for this man. And when he knelt and gently eased her legs out of her jeans, she added incredible.

"Are you sure you can make it on your own?" he asked, folding the jeans and handing them to her.

With all the crazy feelings that she knew to be attraction racing through her, her throw-caution-to-the-wind side, prompted her to say no. She would give anything right now to feel all that male musculature against her body if he carried her upstairs. Her sanity chose not to fail her the one time she wanted it to, and she said 'yes.'

"Okay, I'll go clean up the spill." He smiled slightly, the unexpectedness of it making Jasmine's head whirl a bit. That tiny upward tilt of his mouth relaxed his face and made him look younger, not to mention more approachable. "Thanks for the tea and the sandwich." With a quick squeeze of her arm, he exited the kitchen and headed back to the study.

Jasmine watched him leave, grasping the shoulder he'd touched and wondering why contact with this man made her heart race so wildly.

***

As Adam cleaned up the spill, his thoughts boiled and churned. Something had to be wrong with him. One minute his mind had been on Cheyenne and how much he missed her. The next minute his heart was missing beats when Jasmine cried out and later thundering as he held her close and carried her to the kitchen. He'd fought to stay impersonal, to keep it at employer concerned about employee, when he'd knelt before her and treated her burn. He wouldn't be a man if he didn't notice the flare of her hips and the smoothness of her thighs, so shapely and attractive. But he'd struggled and succeeded in hiding his admiration. He'd been a gentleman, although it had nearly killed him. Adam didn't understand the attraction. He found her aggravating, feisty, and more than once, insubordinate. Yet he felt a clenching in his midsection when she challenged him and a kick in his heartbeat when she entered his study. And, man, when she smiled, his breaths stuttered. The way she made him feel baffled him. He'd had the same feelings for Cheyenne and never thought he'd experience them for someone else.

CHAPTER IV

The next day, Jasmine discovered that Claire could sing. It was Friday and she was doing her Sabbath preparation. The kids had come home early because of a district wide educator in-service training. Mac and Cheese was on the menu, but she didn't remember all the ingredients for making the cheese. She ran upstairs to get the recipe. She paused at the girls' bedroom door at the faint sound of the song "God is." More alto than tenor, the notes came out with a slightly husky but very ear-pleasing quality. Moving with care, Jasmine peered into the room to see Claire belting out the song, a comb her microphone, and with her eyes closed as she held the final note for a long time.

Jasmine forgot she was eavesdropping and exclaimed, "Beautiful! Just beautiful!"

The girl whirled, her expression full of dismay. "How long have you been there?" she demanded accusingly.

"Long enough to know that you have an incredible gift," Jasmine answered, stepping into the room.

Claire turned away. "I haven't sung since mommy died," she admitted. "We used to sing together in church, and it wasn't the same singing by myself."

Jasmine stopped behind her and laid an understanding hand on her shoulder. "Don't you think she would have wanted you to continue?"

She shrugged. "Maybe, but I'm not confident like her. I did it because she was always beside me. I get scared when I stand in front of people."

"I understand that. There's strength in numbers. I mean, if you forget a line, the other person can always carry it too."

Claire spun around. "How'd you know that?" she asked, looking amazed.

"Know what?"

"That I sometimes forget my lines."

She hadn't known. She'd just been sharing words of understanding. "An educated guess," she said, and then added as the idea came to her. "Maybe what you need is another partner."

"Oh, I don't know about that," she doubted, leaning against her dressing table with an uncertain frown.

"Isn't there anybody at church you'd like to sing with?"

The girl shook her head.

"What about your friends?"

Claire laughed a little. It wasn't an amused sound, more one of bitterness. "My school friends don't sing church songs."

"What about your church friends?"

"I don't have any." She lifted a careless shoulder as if she didn't care but wouldn't meet Jasmine's searching gaze. Jasmine knew the lack of friendship at church mattered.

Perching herself at the edge of the queen sized bed Claire shared with Dona, she dug a little into the girl's business. "And why's that?"

"What?"

"Why don't you have church friends?"

Another shrug. "I don't know. The kids there are into cliques, and I don't do cliques. Everybody should be free to talk to whoever they want to without having to be a part of any particular group. I guess I don't fit in with them, so they don't want me as a friend." She tried to make it sound like she didn't care but the last part of her statement sounded hollow and sad.

Jasmine knew all about cliques, not fitting in, and being on the outside. It had happened to her when she'd filed for divorce. The church brethren, most of them, took Simon's side. Despite the truth being that he'd cheated and gotten another woman pregnant, they felt like she should have forgiven him and kept the marriage together. She was that outsider, that girl from New York who broke a southern boy's heart. And Simon, actor that he was, had played it for all it was worth and milked their sympathy. Those women, older and younger, had formed bands of disapproval and ostracized her from group interaction and eventually from that church. So Jasmine didn't like cliques and stayed away from them herself, but she understood that being isolated could be a very sad and lonely business.

She stood. "What if I sang with you, would you sing in church again?"

"You can sing?" Claire looked amazed.

She would just have to prove it. Jasmine cleared her throat and began, "There is a name…"

"OMG! You're mad good," Claire declared when Jasmine finished, her eyes saucer-sized and impressed.

"I'm just grateful for the gift," Jasmine said deprecatingly. "So do you want us to sing together?"

"You bet!"

"When?"

"Tomorrow. I overheard dad say that they didn't have anyone for Special Music tomorrow."

Jasmine paused. So soon? But what did it matter? She didn't have any weekend engagements. Last week she'd visited the Indian Run church and run into Mr. Bump whose interest had bordered on more than brotherly. After the service he'd caught up with her in the parking lot and started a conversation. Jasmine had found his interest in her welfare insincere since he hadn't given her the job that had brought her to Indian Run in the first place. Why was he interested in how she was doing and whether she'd gotten a job after he'd taken away the job she should have had with his school? And then, she'd found out his real reason for coming after her was intimate interest. She'd suspected it from the way his eyes kept sweeping over her face and dropping and lingering below her chin. When he'd asked her to dinner, Jasmine's refusal jumped out as soon as he finished the question. She'd left him looking a little startled at her rapid rejection and quite deflated at her expeditious exit. She was not going back there for a while and chance running into him. "Tomorrow it is," she agreed.

***

Adam had the surprise of his life the next day during the eleven o'clock service. Claire, he'd been expecting, for she told him last night that she would be delivering the Special Music since there was

36

nobody to do it. In his heart he was glad. She hadn't sung in church since Cheyenne died, and it would be good to hear her voice in song again. In a sense it preserved her mother's legacy as Claire carried on the gift that God had blessed them both with.

But what threw him for a curve was when Jasmine Lewis approached the podium and joined Claire. She could sing? For the next few minutes, she answered his silent question and blew him and the congregation away with her and Claire's rendition of The Prayer, Yolanda Adams and Donnie McClurkin style. People were on their feet, applauding and saying 'amen' when the two of them finished. Adam stepped forward and embraced a widely smiling, sparkling-eyed Claire. "I'm proud of you, sweetheart and I love you," he whispered for her ears only.

"I love you too, Daddy," she whispered back and went to her seat. Adam's eyes shifted from his daughter to the woman walking along the side aisle and towards the rear exit. He'd have to talk to Jasmine Lewis later. How had she gotten Claire to do something that she had only ever done with her mother? He wasn't comfortable with the admission, but Jasmine Lewis, despite his initial reservations about her and his reluctance for his mother to leave, had become a blessing to his family.

He wasn't the only one who noticed Jasmine. Scarlet Norman, one of his two female elders, did too. She also noticed how the pastor's gaze tracked the woman with what any female could tell was male interest. She slipped from the sanctuary determined to find out who the competition was.

CHAPTER V

Downstairs in the fellowship hall of the Mt. Calvary SAB Church, the only SAB church, in Mohawk Valley, Jasmine had only one brief moment to share a triumphant hug with Claire before a group of girls converged on them.

"OMG, Claire, we didn't know you could sing like that," a tall, biscuit-colored girl with russet highlights in her hair said. She had led the praise team that morning.

"Girl, you need to sing with us," another one said.

Jasmine slipped away as they surrounded Claire, giving the girl space to talk with her peers. A quick visit to the ladies room and then she would go back into the sanctuary. She was eager to hear Adam King preach.

"You blessed my soul just now. Thank you."

Jasmine looked up from washing her hands to see the reflection of a tall, African-American woman in the mirror. Elegantly dressed in a white, short-sleeved designer suit, she wore a white hat, the brim tipping forward and shadowing her face and the net further blocking a clear look at her features.

"I'm glad you appreciated it," Jasmine answered her, shaking excess water from her hands and drying them. She used paper to turn off the tap and turned to face the woman. They were alone in the ladies room.

"Are you visiting with us today?" the woman asked with a friendly smile.

"Yes."

"Well I hope you'll be back and that you'll sing again."

"Thank you. I'm sure I will be back." Jasmine dropped the paper into the garbage and moved towards the door. The woman walked with her.

Hadn't she come in to use the restroom?

"It's my first time hearing Claire sing too. She has a lovely voice."

"She does. I heard her for the first time yesterday and offered to sing with her when she didn't want to do it alone."

"Oh, that was nice. Are you related?"

"No," Jasmine said, using her elbow to depress the door's handle and push it outwards. "I'm her babysitter."

"Oh, you're watching the children now that Norma left?"

"That's right." Outside the door, the hallway was empty. Jasmine paused and looked up at the woman, seeing for the first time that she was a Lady Di look alike, only a dark version.

"Oh, it's so nice to meet you. Norma and I were friends. I'm Scarlet Norman. You are?"

"Jasmine Lewis." Jasmine shook her hand with a smile. "It's nice to meet you Sis. Norman."

"Scarlet, please," she corrected, with a no-standing-on-ceremony flick of her wrist and a no-time-for-formality look on her face.

Jasmine laughed. "Okay. Call me Jasmine then."

"Good. Now you're both my sister and my visitor," she said with a pleased smile. "How does lunch after church sound?"

What a nice woman. The lunch invitation was thoughtful, but she had cooked. She, Adam, and the kids were having lunch at the house. Adam had told her yesterday that she didn't need to make Sabbath lunch for them. She'd responded that it was a once in a blue moon thing and he shouldn't hold his breath that it would happen again. Her breezy, careless answer had garnered a grin from him, and he'd left the kitchen with two of her homemade cookies while she stared after him, thinking the man would have women flocking behind him if he kept smiling. "May I take a rain check on the offer?" she asked Scarlet Norman. "We're having lunch at Adam's, Pastor King's house today." Jasmine corrected the slip quickly but saw that Scarlet noticed with the way the woman's eyes widened. She needed to stop thinking about him on a first name basis. It was a miracle that she hadn't called him by it to his face yet.

"Certainly. I'll give you a call. I can reach you at Pastor King's house, right?"

Jasmine nodded, and Scarlet walked away with a smile and a wave.

She always tried to take away at least one memorable point from a sermon. Doing that had turned into somewhat of a challenge, for the content of sermons didn't inspire commitment to memory much anymore. Not so with Adam King's message. He didn't have a preaching voice which relieved Jasmine. It turned her off when a pastor had one octave for speaking and another—usually an unbearably loud decibel—for preaching. He delivered the sermon with the same rich cadence with which he spoke—his low pitched, resonant tone elevated in instances to make a point, and then becoming passionate when he captured the magnitude of God and described His glory. Jasmine liked the analogy he used to put God in perspective. He compared the microscopic view to a telescopic view of God. A microscope, he said, gives a false view of something. It enlarges an object, making it seem greater than it is. A telescope puts things into true perspective. It magnifies the stars that look miniature to the human eye, depicting their true size, their mammoth proportions, their vastness and grandeur. "Notice," he told the congregants, "that the microscopic view looks downwards while the telescopic looks upwards." The God we serve is above us. With our naked eyes we cannot see Him, behold Him, or give Him the worship he deserves because we cannot fathom his vastness. But with spiritual binoculars, the telescopic view, we behold him in His infinite, gargantuan glory and know that He is God, greater than the universe, of unfathomable magnitude, and one who is worthy of our praise.

By the time he wrapped up his sermon, the Hallelujahs, Amens, and Praise the Lords, were loud and continuous. The woman next to Jasmine said to her companion, "We had church today." Privately Jasmine echoed the statement. Exiting as they sang the last, hymn, she hurried to the house to heat the food. Adam King had delivered the spiritual food and blessing, now it was her turn to deliver the physical one.

***

After church Adam shook hands with exiting parishioners and

exchanged small talk with them. Greetings over, he went to his study to get his briefcase and head home. His kids had asked to go to friends' homes to eat. It would just be him and Jasmine at the house. His heart skipped at the thought of them alone, and he wondered at his interest in that quarter. Hadn't he signed off any thought of a relationship after Cheyenne, knowing he couldn't risk loving another and losing her as he had his wife? So why did Jasmine Lewis make his mind wander from that commitment? He didn't bother to examine why. He grabbed his briefcase, turned to exit, and ran into Elder Norman.

"Oh, Elder, I'm sorry," he apologized, steadying her with a hand on her arm.

"You're in a hurry, pastor," she stated with a laugh.

"I'm hungry and there's good food at home."

"Well that's always an incentive. I won't keep you then. I just came in to give you this."

She handed him a sheet of paper. "It's the names of members who didn't come today."

Adam took the paper with an appreciative smile. "Thanks, Elder. You make my job so much easier."

"I'm always glad to help." She smiled, pleased. "Enjoy, your lunch," she said, turning to leave.

"Oh, I will," Adam said feelingly. "Jasmine's a good cook."

So it's Jasmine just like how he's Adam to her. How cozy. Hiding her sour thoughts behind a pleasant facade, she turned back to him. "She's a good singer too."

"That caught me by surprise. I thought only Claire was going to sing."

"She's versatile—singer, cook, and babysitter."

"How'd you know she's watching my kids?" He looked at her quizzically.

"I met her in the ladies room and introduced myself."

"Oh."

"She seems really nice. Her accent's a little different though."

Adam hadn't really noticed. "Different how?"

"A little bit southern."

"She taught in Florida for five years." He remembered that from her resume.

Scarlet stepped closer to get information on the opposition.

"She teaches?" *Why was she babysitting?* "Did she stop teaching?"

"My understanding is that she was offered a position at the Indian Run School and when she got here it was rescinded."

Scarlet was dying to know the details behind that but didn't want him to get suspicious of her unnatural interest. So she just said, "Oh, that's too bad, but that loss is your gain."

Adam hadn't thought about it like that, but Elder Norman had a point. "You're right about that," he said. "It's my gain in more than one way and right now, I'm about to gain some good food."

They both laughed. He waved goodbye and headed out of his office. Scarlet Norman watched his retreating back and thought that she had a whole lot of research to do tonight on a teacher from Florida named, Jasmine Lewis. The woman had to have taught in the Florida SAB school system if she'd had a job offer at Indian Run School. She had a girlfriend in Jacksonville who taught within that system. Winona might know Jasmine Lewis. As she left the office, she wondered what she would find. Lots of ammunition she hoped.

CHAPTER VI

Jasmine had the table set and food heating on the stove by the time she heard the garage doors lift downstairs. She still couldn't wear jeans. Shorts weren't an alternative, not with Adam in the house, so she settled for a knee length cotton A-line skirt and a camisole. It was hot today, although it was comfortable in the house since Adam had left the A/C running.

She descended the stairs to find Adam in shirtsleeves in the kitchen opening pots.

"Where are the kids?"

"Went to friends' homes," he said turning around.

Hadn't Claire said she didn't have any? But the way those girls flocked her earlier, Jasmine had suspected the girl's friendless condition was about to change. Apparently change had come quicker than she expected. So it was just her and Adam. Her heart thumped. Her stomach rolled. Oh, oh. It was a big kitchen, but suddenly the walls seemed to shrink and the air right along with it. Jasmine realized that they had never been truly alone in the house. The thought excited and scared her at the same time. This charge she felt around him was one sided. His circumspect behavior towards her never changed; so the attraction in the air had a single source—her.

She gripped the island's counter, the rectangular slab of granite over cupboards separating them across the kitchen. He was watching her, studying her face...and her figure—not at all circumspectly. The latter awareness made her breathless. His brown eyes filled with lazy interest. He moved away from the stove—his tread purposeful, his progress measured—and paused a barely respectable distance away from her.

Jasmine looked a long way up. Her world almost went black at the fullness of the smile he sent towards her. An electric volt had never hit her before, but this was close.

"Thanks for singing with Claire today."

"It was nothing." She sounded like she could use a respirator.

"It was a big deal to me and to her. It's a God-given gift that had rusted from disuse. You resurrected it. Thanks."

Jasmine smiled, not knowing what to say to the depth of his appreciation.

"Are you up for a picnic?"

Jasmine blinked at the unexpectedness of the question. She tried to tell herself that they had to eat and with it being such a beautiful day, an al fresco meal appealed. It was the sole explanation for the question. It wasn't an invitation and definitely not a date. At the end of the rationalization, she didn't believe it. His interest signals were subtle but they were there. That meant this was an offer to go out on a date. She passed her tongue across her lips. "Are you inviting me to one?" Her eyelashes swept up and down fast. Some might call it flirting. For her: an involuntary action. Right.

"Are you accepting?"

"I might…on one condition."

"And what is that?"

Had his cadence dropped? Had he moved closer?

"That you switch this," she touched his shirt sleeve, "for something more comfortable."

"Well now," he rested an elbow on the counter, the move tilting him slightly closer. Jasmine could smell the musk mixed with the fruit fragrance of his cologne. Delicious! "That all depends on if it's worth the trouble. Are we dining in or out?"

If this wasn't flirting, Jasmine didn't know what was. Enjoying every minute of something she never thought she would again after what she'd experienced with Simon, she murmured, "Depends. Are you changing or not?"

That slow, devastating smile unfurled again—the one that transformed his face to youthful and shot desire through her like a hot flash. "I'll be right back," he promised, his words a sensual rumble across Jasmine's ears. And then he reached out and brushed his thumb across her cheek, the movement slow and caressing. "Cookie crumb," he explained with a smile as he headed towards the stairs, leaving Jasmine fighting to stay on her feet at the tenderness of his touch and knowing for sure she hadn't had any cookies today.

***

They went to a place called Rock Point Park. Crowded though it was on a Saturday afternoon, Adam promised picnic privacy and delivered. He followed a footpath eastwards and deeper into the park and climbed up two inclines. The second crested on a mini hill. He spread the blanket they had brought on the ground and set the basket in the middle. Jasmine toed off her sneakers and knelt on the blanket, following his example.

"Will you pray or shall I?" he asked.

"I'll do it." She offered up a short prayer, asking a blessing on the meal. At the end Adam said amen first and fast, obviously hungry. She started praying again, thanking God for the fresh air, sunshine, flowers, trees, and everything else in nature. Jasmine cracked her eyes open, continuing her list to see Adam watching her in dismay. She burst out laughing.

He grimaced. "You're terrible. You shouldn't play pranks on a hungry man."

Jasmine opened the basket, and they helped themselves. She'd packed a salad, rolls, Mac and Cheese, string beans, broccoli, tofu meatballs, and the meatless vegetarian chicken she'd prepared yesterday. Adam didn't know about it, but she'd made a cake too and had put a few slices in the bottom of the basket. It would be a nice surprise. She'd figured out that he liked sweets. Half the cookies she'd left cooling on the counter on Friday night had disappeared come Sabbath morning. They'd all been there when the kids had gone to bed, so the culprit had to be him.

"You look different," she observed, her eyes moving over his close fitting T-Shirt and black Levi's. She'd only ever seen him in suits.

"Different how?" he asked around a mouthful of salad.

"More relaxed and at ease. Less austere."

"Less austere? I didn't know I looked that way."

"Well you're always in a suit and tie and to tell you the truth, today is the first time that I've really seen you smile—the second

45

time, actually. You smiled on Thursday when you played doctor for me. But today is the *most* I've seen you smile."

His lips tightened, and Jasmine wondered what she'd said to make his mouth turn uptight. What he said next was a non-sequitur, and she had a feeling it was deliberate. "By the way, how's your leg?"

"It's healing nicely, thank you. So why don't you smile much, Pastor King?"

For some reason it felt awkward calling him that, especially in the relaxed outdoor setting. He must have sensed it too, for he said, "Call me Adam."

"If you insist." She sent him a mischief-filled smile, but he didn't return it. "Smile Adam. It's the Sabbath. God has given us sunshine and clear skies. We have food and best of all we're alive."

Adam set his plate down, pushed to his feet, and paced some steps away. He very much was that—alive—and enjoying that life with someone else right now while his wife was very much dead. What was he doing out with another woman? What was he doing wanting somebody else? This picnic was a mistake. He felt as if he were betraying his wife's memory. Still he craved Jasmine's companionship and enjoyed her reciprocated interest.

Oh, boy. She had definitely said something wrong. Jasmine put her own plate down and scrambled to her feet. She came up behind him, wanting to restore the ease between them. "I'm sorry. I don't know what I said, but whatever it is, I'm sorry. You don't have to smile if you don't feel like it, but it makes you so much more approachable and nice…attractive too."

With their earlier flirtation, Adam pretty much understood that she returned his interest. Her admission just now surprised him though, although it shouldn't. Most women would be too shy to say something like that, but Jasmine Lewis spoke her mind. That he knew from experience when she tried to tell him how to be a parent. She was different from Cheyenne who had not been the outspoken type. Physically and in personality the two were polar opposites. But Cheyenne was dead and Jasmine was alive, and right now as the sunlight fell on her face and illuminated her beauty, *he* felt very much alive. Her allure appealed to him, built desire to taste lips glistening in the light, to experience what a live, warm-blooded male typically did when a woman as desirable at Jasmine Lewis stood so close.

He turned slowly and captured her gaze. A slight shift forward and his body touched hers. She should have stepped back because he'd breached her personal space. Instead she held her ground and held his gaze, the want in his heart reflected in her eyes.

Jasmine stopped breathing. Survival necessitated that she start back up again. Her lips parted to accommodate freer flow of air. Adam was close. He was touching her. Pretty soon he'd be kissing her. His body blocked the sun. His head was descending too slowly so she went on tiptoes and met him half way. He tasted like raisin and Italian dressing—sweet, tangy and very good. One arm circled her waist and the other cupped her cheek. His mouth moved over hers gently, kissing with a tenderness that left her aching from the softness of his touch. Jasmine shifted in his arms, sliding her arms up his chest and linking her hands behind his neck. Anchored now, she returned his kiss and kept the connection light and searching like he was doing. His body was solid and sculpted—the feel of his chest against hers like rock against a bed of grass. She let her fingers feather down the side of his neck and felt muscles bunch at her caress.

A sound, long and low like it started from his extremity and raised to his throat, vibrated in the quiet between them, the echo of it achy and needy. He gathered her closer and took the kiss deeper. Jasmine accommodated the increased pressure of his lips over hers. Searching transitioned to investigative quest—a determination to know her beyond a surface touch. At her subtle accommodation, he augmented the intensity of the intimate contact, giving Jasmine an experience that was exquisite, delicious, explosive, and one that left her wanting much more of his mouth and the magic of it when the kiss ended.

It took a while for the exterior sounds—the picnickers below, the birds chirping in the trees, the wind rustling leaves—to supersede the thunder of her heart in her ears. Adam's heart was pounding against her shoulder, and his breathing was as ragged as hers. She didn't speak because she couldn't, and he was silent with the same problem it seemed. They'd crossed the employer, employee line, but she didn't care if it didn't matter to him. She knew with the flirtation from earlier that this had been possible.

He tipped her chin up. She searched his face and saw wonder and wariness in his gaze. What was he thinking?

"Thanks for making me feel alive," he whispered before stepping away and moving back to the blanket.

It took Jasmine a little while longer to command her emotions back under perfect control. When she turned around, he was eating the salad he'd left earlier. She made him feel alive? She hadn't known he'd been feeling dead. Is that why he didn't smile much? Because he felt dead inside? But why? This wasn't the right time to ask questions. Jasmine was intuitive enough to know that, but curiosity rode her relentlessly.

***

Jasmine had the right footwear and she was fairly fit, but they had been walking for a while and the terrain was all uphill. This nature walk was a real educational experience. Adam knew his trees. She had to give him that. Now she knew the trees she kept seeing with the blade like leaves were locusts, and she recognized birch by the razor edges of the leaves. She could also tell the difference between pines, and for the most part she identified the difference between those trees, firs, and spruce, when Adam asked her. After forty-five minutes, she planted her hands on her hips and stopped on the footpath that kept winding uphill.

"Okay, Adam. This is as far as I'm going. My food's digested now."

"But the best part is just around the corner."

"You've been telling me that for the past fifteen minutes," she said accusingly.

He grinned, unrepentant.

Jasmine decided not to comment on his smiles anymore, choosing instead to revel quietly in them as they appeared.

"Come on, I'll help you the rest of the way," he offered, slipping a supportive arm around her waist and propelling her forward.

Jasmine went willingly, the feel of his fingers against her side sending flutters across her middle.

He didn't misspeak this time. The best part *was* around the corner, and it was a spectacular view of the surrounding Seneca Mountain communities laid out in the valley below. Adam shifted her in front of him to give another couple a place at the railing to admire the view. Jasmine swallowed when his warm body touched hers from behind. She felt his chest against her back. She willed herself not to sink into him. The desire to do that escalated with every second of his sweet proximity. Maybe she shouldn't have let him kiss her. Then she'd still be in ignorance about the magnificence of his muscles and how stimulating they felt on contact. "That's Indian Run," he pointed to settlements on the left. "Way north is Heart Haven. Below that is Mohawk Valley, and to the right is Mountain Spring."

Vibrant, healthy, and beautiful. From up here the trees and vegetation formed a continuous canopy of green, interrupted by buildings. "It's awesome," she said.

"I think so too. It kind of makes me feel like I'm on top of the world and like nothing can touch me this far up. It's a powerful feeling."

"I thought only God could do that." She tipped her head back to look at him.

He searched her face as if seeking the intent behind her statement. "I said the place makes me *feel like* I'm on top of the world. God *puts* us on top."

"I see the difference." Jasmine smiled. "One's illusion; the other is reality."

"Something like that." He shifted to stand beside her and lean his elbows on the rail. Jasmine immediately missed his warmth at her back. "How long have you been SAB?"

"Since I was fifteen. I got baptized then. You?"

"Raised in the church. Got baptized when I was ten." He watched a raven fly across the valley. "Did you ever stop believing?"

Jasmine frowned. What a strange question? "Apostatize you mean?"

"That too." He shifted his gaze from the valley to her, his eyes intent like her response mattered.

What was going on in Adam's head?

"No, I never stopped believing—not truly, no." She shook her head.

"Truly, you said. Why the qualifier?"

"Why is it important?" She wanted to know the intent behind these questions because this didn't seem like light conversation. But she was stalling too because she didn't want to talk about her divorce. Going through it and experiencing infidelity had shaken her confidence in God a little. She had asked 'why?' There had been many days where she didn't want to pray, hadn't prayed, but she hadn't really stopped believing in God's presence or in His care. At the height of her pain she just wanted it to go away, wanted her husband back, wanted her marriage back, and her perfect life back. Her mother had been a rock for her then, her go-to person when she wanted to cry and scream and vent at life's cruelty. In bad times, everybody needed a human somebody especially when your problems put God out of perspective. She knew what she was talking about. Been there, done that.

"It's not important," Adam answered with a shrug as if it weren't, but she didn't believe him.

"Okay. There was one time in my life when my faith got shaky. It was a difficult circumstance—something I never believed would happen to me." He was watching her as if expecting more. He wasn't going to get anymore. They didn't know each other that deeply for her to hang all her business out there.

"So what strengthened your faith?"

"His Word—God's promise that he wouldn't give me more than I can bear but would make a way of escape."

"I've read that. My thing is, how long do you have to wait for that 'escape'? Sometimes it's so long that you stop believing relief will come."

She didn't know how to answer him. He was the preacher. Shouldn't he know?

"I'll read it again tonight," he said after a while. "It worked for you. Maybe it'll work for me this time."

Jasmine sensed that something was making his faith waver. It helped to share sometimes. She put an offer out there. "I'm a good listener if you need to talk."

He studied her, his gaze contemplative. "Thanks. If you're as good a listener as you are a talker, maybe I'll take you up on it sometime."

"Okay, Adam, the ball's in your court."

"Is it?"

The subtle shift in his cadence cued her in that the topic had changed. When his gaze dropped to her mouth, she saw his thoughts. Her tongue darted out to moisten lips gone dry from more than the sun's heat. "Absolutely," she answered breathlessly.

He smiled and reached for her hand. "Let's head back. It's a bit too hot out here. Don't you think?"

CHAPTER VII

Jasmine woke up on Sunday morning to rain drops pelting the roof and sliding down her windows' panes. Sundays were usually slow days for her. The weather alone made it a lazy day. She burrowed deeper under the sheets. She wasn't the only late riser on the last day of the weekend. The King family tended to sleep in too—Adam, Jr. in particular. Last week, he'd stumbled out of his room at two o'clock in the afternoon.

Her phone rang. Jasmine thought about not answering it. It might be her mother. Throwing back the sheet, she crawled across the bed and reached for the device on the night stand.

"Good morning, mom."

"Hi, sweetheart. How are you?"

"Fine and in bed."

"You seem to spend a lot of time in your room."

"No, mom," Jasmine laughed. "You always call me when I'm in bed."

"Speaking of which, I sent you a comforter and some throw pillows that will complement the accents in your room." Acquilla Lewis was into home décor.

"Accents? Mom, the walls are peach and the curtains deep green."

"There you go. Accents. You said the furniture—dressing table, night stand and armoire are white, right?"

52

"Right."

"So I sent a patchwork quilt comforter with all three colors and green pillows."

"Thanks, mom. I know they are beautiful, and I will enjoy them."

"So, how are you and your employer getting along?"

Jasmine smiled. She'd told her mother about the spirited interview. Acquilla had been expecting her to get fired.

"So far so good."

"Norma showed me a picture of him. He's handsome."

Oh no, she wasn't entertaining that line of conversation. She changed the topic completely. "How's Jim?" Jim was her mother's fiancé. At sixty-four, Acquilla often laughed at the fact that she was engaged in her senior years. Jasmine's dad died ten years ago.

"He's fine sweetheart and right here."

Jasmine heard her mother tell Jim that she said 'hello.'

"He says 'hi.' Now, don't you think Adam King is handsome?"

She sighed. "Mom, I don't think it's appropriate for me to view him like that. He's my boss."

"Honey, ladies fall in love with their bosses all the time. He's single, you're single. What's the big deal?"

"I'm not looking for anybody mother."

"You don't have to be looking. I wasn't. Sometimes it just happens, especially if the circumstances are conducive to romance and your circumstances certainly are."

"My circumstances?"

"Yours and his, honey. You're a pretty girl; he's a handsome guy. You're both healthy and living in close proximity. Attraction is a natural thing."

It was, but Jasmine wasn't about to admit that to her mother who had high hopes of her finding 'a decent, God-fearing, and loving man.' Acquilla hadn't thought those things of Simon. Jasmine wished she hadn't overridden her mother's objections to that match. Anyway, water under the bridge.

"Mom, you have such a creative mind. You should write love stories."

"Why should I when I'm living one?"

Jasmine heard a giggle and a long smooching sound. Lord, her mother was kissing Jim.

"Okay, mom, this is getting icky. If you're going to lock lips, get off the phone," Jasmine joked.

"At my age we kiss conservatively, not lock lips. I leave that up to you young people."

What she and Adam shared yesterday had been shy of lip-locking. The memory of it had occupied her dreams last night. She wouldn't mind doing some actual lip-locking with him though.

"Mom, I'm thirty-four. That's not young."

"Adam's forty-two."

Jasmine rolled her eyes, and then got suspicious. "How do you know that?"

"Norma and I've kept in touch since we ran into each other."

"And I can just imagine that Adam and I are the center of all your conversations."

"Pretty much," Acquilla confessed without shame. "So he's Adam now? Isn't that a bit familiar, since he *is* your boss like you pointed out earlier?"

Busted. Jasmine covered her eyes. She could hear the laughter in her mother's voice. The first name thing had caught up with her again. "Mom, I've got to go. I've been invited to a picnic, and I have to get ready." Scarlet Norman had invited her to a pool side picnic at her house.

"Go, go," Acquilla shooed her off the line, still laughing. "Remember you can run but you can't hide and what's done in the dark will come to the light. Isn't that the name of a Tyler Perry movie or something?"

"Bye, mom." Jasmine rang off chuckling.

***

"Where are you going?"

Jasmine stopped stuffing things into her tote and threw a glance over her shoulder. Claire had poked her head around the door.

"To a pool party," she answered the girl.

Claire's eyes went wide with interest. "Ooh, may I come?"

"If your dad says yes," Jasmine answered, thinking that she would have to call Scarlet to see if it were okay. She didn't think it would be a problem though.

"He took the boys for piano lessons, but I can call him."

"Do that," Jasmine instructed, reaching for her phone to place that call to Scarlet. "What about Dona? Did she go with them?"

54

"No. I'm watching her. Can she come too?"

Jasmine smiled. From one to two to three. "As long as your dad clears it," she told Claire.

Five minutes later Claire came back with her sister. "Dad said yes," she announced.

Scarlet had said yes too. "Great," Jasmine said. "You'll need your swimsuits."

"We're wearing them," Dona said.

"You changed fast."

"We love swimming and haven't been in a while, so we're looking forward to this," Claire explained. She looked at the bed. "That's pretty." She pointed to the fuchsia blouse on the bed.

Jasmine picked up the top she'd discarded earlier.

"May I try it on?" Claire asked, admiring the garment.

"Sure," Jasmine agreed and offered it to her.

She accepted it with care and handled it as if it were priceless. She changed her top and dropped the blouse over her head. The one shoulder Jersey top looked cute and sporty on her, and Claire filled out the bust better than Jasmine. The attached ruffle at the garment's hem made the blouse flirty and feminine. Jasmine told her to wear it. An effusive hug declared that she fulfilled the girl's private hope. By the time they left, Claire had borrowed sunglasses and fuchsia-colored wedge pumps. Dona, not wanting to be left out, took a floppy straw hat that Jasmine had on top of the dressing table.

CHAPTER VIII

The weather cleared and sunshine poured down instead of rain. Jasmine followed her GPS directly to Scarlet Norman's ranch styled house. In this part of Mohawk Valley, neighbors were further apart than where Adam and his family lived. Yet the ampleness of the property acreage was the same. About ten cars were parked before the house and on the front lawn. Jasmine pulled up behind a KIA jeep. She got the basket from the trunk while Claire took the tote with all their swim suits. Dona skipped ahead free and unencumbered as a bird and eager to get in the pool.

Jasmine stepped up on the pretty white porch with pink and blue balusters, supporting the white railing. Scarlet Norman's porch was a horticultural heaven. Potted croutons resided on either side of the top steps and on both sides of the front door. Bacopa, pretty and pinkish-purple, as well as trailing fuchsia hung from pots suspended from the porch's ceiling. Jasmine felt like she could sit in one of the rockers and enjoy nature safe from the Lyme and dog ticks common to the outdoors in this area. The porch garden created a relaxing and inviting atmosphere. The welcome mat and Scarlet Norman's wide smile and enthusiastic hugs when she opened the door did the rest.

"I'm so glad you made it, Jasmine and that you brought the girls," she greeted, embracing each of them enthusiastically. "Come in and come out back."

Jasmine followed her across glazed cream ceramic tiles, bypassing a living room, dining room, and kitchen to a stone-tiled back porch strewn with summer recliners and chairs. The huge pool was full of teenage girls, some of whom she'd seen at church yesterday. A group of about ten women sat to the left talking and laughing, each of them in swimsuits that Jasmine thought of as breathless bikinis. The blessing was that it was an all girls affair.

The girls in the pool waved Claire over.

Jasmine wondered if there were kids Dona's age. She noticed how the child's face fell as she looked around and didn't see peers.

"Tammy and Petra just went inside to change into swimsuits," Scarlet told Dona.

The girl's face brightened at once. Jasmine figured they were Dona's friends. She ran over to her sister, plucked her one piece swimsuit from the bag, and ran inside to find Tammy and Petra.

"Let me introduce you to the big girls, Jasmine," Scarlet said, taking her hand. "Everybody, meet my friend, Jasmine. She's new to Mohawk Valley. Let's make her feel welcome so she doesn't miss Florida."

Jasmine glanced at Scarlet in surprise. How did the woman know where she was from?

"Pastor King told me," Scarlet explained, seeing her expression.

The women introduced themselves, and Jasmine tried to keep up with the names.

"You take a seat right here beside, Tracey, and I'll take that basket from you. You didn't have to bring anything but thanks."

"So where in Florida are you from?" Tracey asked as soon as Scarlet stepped away.

"Fort Lauderdale."

Scarlet came back and set a glass of lemonade before her. Jasmine murmured her thanks.

"I understand that you're a teacher," Scarlet said, pulling up a chair and sitting down.

Jasmine supposed Pastor King had told her that too. She didn't have anything to hide, but she wondered what else he had told this woman about her. She nodded, acknowledging Scarlet's statement.

"Keisha teaches at Mohawk Valley high," Scarlet volunteered, pointing to a mocha colored woman whose dampened hair said she'd already been in the pool. "Eva is a teacher too, but she's home with kids right now." A young Hispanic-looking woman with a build as slight as Jasmine's smiled and waved.

"Where do you teach?" Keisha asked, picking a strawberry from the fruit platter on the table and popping it into her mouth.

"I'm not teaching right now."

"She's babysitting for Pastor King," Scarlet inserted, and Jasmine started wondering why she kept volunteering information that wasn't solicited. But maybe she was trying to get the other women to know her. Equal flow of information would have been preferable though. Jasmine didn't know a thing about them except their names.

"Don't you find him attractive?" Gwen, a chest-blessed woman to the left asked.

Jasmine contained a smile, not wanting to encourage curiosity. It was the conversation earlier with her mother all over again. "I've been so busy that I haven't really noticed."

"Come on," the woman called Dahlia teased with a sly look— Jasmine remembered her name because of her floral printed swimwear. "There is no one here who doesn't notice that our pastor is dynamic in his preaching and his physique."

The women hooted and laughed. Jasmine lowered her eyes to hide her amusement, but a grin escaped.

"Oh, leave her alone," Scarlet protested, hugging Jasmine in a protective way. "Maybe the girl is married, and has eyes for one man only—her husband."

"I'm not," Jasmine was quick to point out.

"So you must notice how fine he looks," Dahlia pressed.

Jasmine wondered if she were interested in Adam, what with the way she fixated on this line of talk. "He's nice, but he's my employer."

"Girl, there is no law against a little office interaction," Dahlia declared. "Or in this case home interaction."

"Unless, you're down on men like me." This came from a woman sitting outside the circle. She had on huge sunglasses and a floppy straw hat, blocking Jasmine's view of her face.

"Oh, stop, Gretta," Dahlia waved a dismissive hand her way. Everybody knows you hate men since your divorce."

Jasmine knew it was probably just friendly ribbing on the part of friends, but with her own divorce, especially in the immediate months following it, she'd been emotionally raw and had wanted nothing to do with men. Maybe Gretta's divorce was recent. Either way, Jasmine felt that Dahlia should be a bit more sensitive.

"Oh, no, honey, I love them," Gretta drawled. "I just love myself more." With a cheeky grin and a lemonade salute to Dahlia, she crossed her legs and sipped her drink like she couldn't care less.

"Amen to that," Jasmine murmured, liking Gretta's answer and attitude.

Curious eyes zeroed in on her.

"You talk like you have experience. Have you been divorced?"

The nosy question came from Tracey. She looked around the table. Everybody was looking at her, inquisitive about her reply. Jasmine didn't want these women, no matter how jovial and friendly, to know her business, but didn't see how she could get around a truthful reply.

"Yes, I have," she said quietly.

"Good for you, baby," Gretta hailed her from the other side. "He didn't deserve you. If he was anything like mine, he stepped out on you with some younger thing and got her pregnant."

The bulls-eye conclusion knocked a gasp from Jasmine.

"Enough, Gretta," Scarlet put in when every eye made Jasmine the center of their focus again. "Now, Jasmine, let me tell you about these girls since they seem to know a bit more about you. Dahlia here is a widow and on the prowl, so if you like the pastor, watch her."

Everybody laughed, including Dahlia. Jasmine was grateful to Scarlet for taking the focus off her.

"Eva is the newlywed amongst us—two years now. She has two kids—back to back you can imagine," Scarlet went on which generated more laughter. Eva blushed and laughed shyly.

By the time Scarlet was done, Jasmine found out that five of the women were married, and of the other five, one was divorced— Gretta—while the others were waiting for Mr. Right. Jasmine wondered if one of them was truly interested in Adam King. With the scarcity of marriageable men, she wouldn't be surprised if all the single ones were—joking aside.

The teenagers left the pool and congregated on their side of the back yard set up with their own food table and lounge chairs. Scarlet challenged the women to a breast stroke race. They all headed for the pool except Gretta. Jasmine rose to get her suit from the tote that Claire had.

"Stay awhile," Gretta invited. "Let's chat. I can't go in. It's that time of the month."

Jasmine made an understanding sound. The woman needed company. She understood, but she wanted to swim. Besides, she didn't want to participate in a fishing expedition, and Jasmine had a suspicion that it was what Gretta had in mind. She was the fish; and Gretta would be doing the fishing.

"Let me change. The water looks inviting, and I really want to take a dip. Maybe we can talk afterwards."

"Okay. There's a bathroom to the left of the dining room."

Five hours later after lots of dips, pool volleyball, shoot ball—a water version of basketball—ping pong, water hockey, and lots of hilarity, everybody got out of the pool and helped with the clean up.

Jasmine waited until everyone had changed to get out of her swimsuit into street clothes. There were three bathrooms; but with a crowd of women taking anywhere from seven to fifteen minutes to put on their public faces, it was a long wait.

She exited the bathroom and headed for the stairs. Almost there, she paused when she heard her name from behind a door she assumed was a bedroom. Probably she would have kept going, but the scornful stress on the syllables stopped her.

"What does Jasmine have that I don't?"

Scarlet spoke those words. From the venom in them and the temper in her voice, Jasmine could imagine the curl of disdain on her lips.

"She's in his house and you aren't." This came from Gretta, and her voice shook a bit with amusement.

"Well if I have my way she won't be there long."

Say what?

"And just how do you propose to get her out?"

"I'm working on a plan."

"While she's in there working on him," Gretta remarked, rubbing it in.

"Will you be quiet? Whose side are you on anyway?" Scarlet sounded petulant.

"I'm just showing you what you're up against. Knowing the enemy's strengths and your weaknesses make for better strategic planning," Gretta said. "If I were you, I'd find a way to make it imperative for her to leave."

"I have to think of something fast," Scarlet said. "When I spoke to Winona last night I thought I'd get dirt on her."

Winona? Who was that?

"Instead, all you found out is that she divorced her husband for impregnating a younger woman."

Jasmine slapped a hand over her mouth to stifle her astonishment. From Gretta's statement just now, her earlier remark about divorce was based on prior knowledge of Jasmine's divorce. And Scarlet had gotten that information from someone named Winona. She had also tried to dig up dirt on Jasmine because she wanted Adam for herself. What a wicked woman, Jasmine thought. All of them were evil.

"You suggested that I make it imperative for her to leave, Gretta. Do you have ideas on how to do that?" Scarlet asked.

"Gretta always has ideas when it comes to making men do things."

That sounded like Tracey.

"I'm not trying to make Adam do anything. It's that woman I want out of his house."

From 'my friend' earlier to 'that woman.' What a fraud! Jasmine fumed.

"How about if you fix it so that he has no choice but to fire her?" Gretta asked.

A short silence followed in which Jasmine held her breath.

"Tell me more," Scarlet spoke, her voice lower than before. Jasmine strained her ears to hear.

"Told you she had ideas," Tracey said.

"Gretta, you're a crafty one," Dahlia spoke now.

"Had to be honey. How do you think I'm raking in so much alimony from Ricky?"

They laughed again and then Gretta spoke, "I'll call you later, Scarlet, and let you know more details. See you."

Jasmine hurried quietly down the stairs, her mind whirling with the discovery that the women she'd met today were not all friendly. And the one she thought was the nicest, Scarlet Norman, hated her with a passion.

CHAPTER IX

Claire and Dona chattered non-stop on the ride home about what a great time they had. Jasmine responded when they pulled her into the conversation but couldn't summon even a shadow of the enthusiasm they felt. Her enjoyment of the day fizzled out after what she'd overheard. Scarlet Norman was interested in Adam King. Jasmine found that the only plausible conclusion for the woman wanting to get her out of his house. Somehow Scarlet saw her as competition and wanted her out of the way. With the interest Adam had shown yesterday at the park, Jasmine wondered if he were even interested in the woman. Maybe Scarlet Norman's interest was one-sided, but then again, maybe not.

She remembered her marriage to Simon. He'd been married to her when he fooled around with Rhonda. Because of that experience, she wouldn't swear to a man's faithfulness. She didn't know Adam King; and even if she did, she wouldn't lay her head down on the chopping block. No sir, not for any man would she do that. Nine times out of ten, a woman would lose her head right along with her heart.

At the house, she parked in her usual spot on the right side of the two car garage. When she got down from the Ford focus, Dona and Claire converged on her and hugged her tightly.

"Thanks, Jasmine, for taking us along. We really had a great time," Claire spoke for both of them. "And thanks so much for the loan of the clothes. They're really cool. All the girls thought so."

Jasmine laughed, the first real one since the bad aftertaste left by those hypocritical wretches. "I hope you didn't tell them you borrowed the clothes."

"Of course not!" Claire exclaimed as if the very idea were poisonous.

"Well you're welcome to shop in my closet if you have a need. Just return items when you're done and in one piece."

"I will Jasmine." Claire smiled happily and hugged her again. "You're amazing."

"And a lot of fun," Dona added.

Jasmine batted her lashes to clear the sudden tears welling in her eyes, touched by their genuine appreciation. "Oh, girls, you're incredible too, and having you along made it fun."

"We should go shopping together," Claire suggested as the three of them walked arm in arm to the front door.

"We will as soon as I get paid."

"Do you need an advance? I can tell daddy to give you one."

"Oh, no, no." Jasmine was quick to put that suggestion to sleep. With the earnest look on Claire's face, she had no doubt that the girl would follow through. "I'm good. It's just that I run on a budget, and shopping—clothes shopping—can wait until I get paid."

"Daddy calls it deferred gratification," Claire said with a grimace. Obviously she didn't believe in it.

"Waiting to acquire something until you can financially afford it is good. It stops you from getting into debt. Your father is a wise man."

"Do you notice anything else about him besides that?" Dona asked out of the blue.

They were at the front door, and Claire was opening it with her key. "Like what?" Jasmine asked, throwing the girl a confused look.

"Like how handsome he is," Dona said, her eyes twinkling with mischief. Jasmine blushed.

"I-I..." Jasmine trailed off. She didn't know what to say. Well she did, but she didn't want to voice her thoughts. "He's nice," she finally admitted lamely.

"But not handsome?" Claire asked with a frown as if she could not believe that there was a female who didn't think her father attractive. She unlocked the door, but nobody moved to go inside.

Jasmine chose her words carefully. "Girls, your dad *is* an attractive man. I think every woman can see that." Those at the pool party in particular, she thought. "But he's my employer, and it wouldn't be proper for me to be thinking about him in that way." Why was that line sounding like a broken record? She'd said it to her mom, those women, and now the girls—all in the same day. No wonder!

"That's good," Claire said, smiling now, "because he finds you attractive too."

Jasmine stared nonplussed at the confident declaration. What had they seen or heard? As far as she recalled, neither she nor Adam had behaved in a way, at least not before the kids, to make them think that they were interested in each other. She passed her tongue across her lips, "Ah, Claire, how do you know that?"

Claire blushed a bit and looked down. "Well, according to Adam, dad looks at you the way he used to look at mom," she revealed shyly.

Her heart skipped. "And how did he used to look at her?" The question came out as hushed as the revelation.

"I know," Dona put in eagerly, "like she was his favorite dessert."

Jasmine didn't find her words immediately. Wow, she thought. She hadn't caught that look but wished she had. She laughed softly and brushed the observation aside with, "I'm sure you're mistaken, girls. Your dad and I just met. He wouldn't be looking at me that way so fast."

Claire and Dona looked at her, their faces mirroring disbelief. Jasmine wasn't sure *she* believed it. She pushed the door open, and they entered the house.

***

Jasmine decided to have an early night. Two hours after she and the girls returned, she got in bed and picked up the latest in the Tracey Barnes detective series. Her phone beeped with an incoming text. Jasmine reached for the phone on the night stand and frowned at the terse message of the text. *Meet me in the study at 9 pm sharp. Adam.*

She knew she was in trouble from the tone of the text and the location for the meeting. She was starting to see the study as her crime correction center. The last time he'd summoned her there had been to accuse and chastise her. She had a feeling this time wouldn't be different. What was she guilty of now?

CHAPTER X

Jasmine changed into a polka dot print knee-length dress with spaghetti straps. The flared skirt, close fitting waistline, and padded bust gave it a 50's night-on-the-town-look. She added a short sleeved bolero because she felt a bit exposed. She pushed her feet into white flip-flops with lilies on the straps, headed down the stairs, and knocked on the study door at precisely nine o'clock.

She straightened her spine at the stern command to enter. Jasmine stepped into the study, her body braced for battle. Adam King wasn't sitting behind his desk as she expected. Rather he was standing and leaning against it, his arms folded across his chest. With his gaze trained on her unwaveringly, he looked more forbidding than she had ever seen him.

She closed the door, moved forward two steps, and stopped— not just because her knees felt rubbery, but from a distance his height was not as overwhelming to her mere five feet. Jasmine moistened her lips. "You wanted to see me?" she asked, glad she sounded confident, although she didn't feel that way at all.

He didn't respond right away, and Jasmine's fortitude started flagging as the silence continued. "I got a call," he finally began, "that you took my children to a pool party this afternoon."

That was her crime? That's why he was watching her with that unyielding and accusatory expression? Because she'd taken the girls to have a good time?

"At first I was going to overlook it as ignorance, but when I heard that you kept them at the party after you were told that I don't allow my children around any large body of water, I decided that hiring you was a mistake I should never have made."

Hold up, hold up. Jasmine raised a finger in the air. "Wait one minute. You are reprimanding me based on hearsay? Some mysterious *liar* told you I made the girls stay at the party after knowing you didn't want them there. You didn't think to verify if the so-called facts were true?" Jasmine stopped and glared at him, angry that he'd condemned her without seeking to find out first if she were innocent. And to think she'd started viewing him as a nice guy. First impressions where Adam King was concerned were lasting ones. He was every bit as hard, harsh, and judgmental as she had thought him to be. "I'd like to know who fed you that lie. First of all I didn't know you didn't want your kids around water. If it were that important, why didn't the girls tell me?"

"Because they love to swim."

"So why don't you want them to?"

"That's none of your business," he said coldly. "And it has nothing to do with the issue at hand which is your jeopardizing my children's safety."

Say what? Jasmine searched his face, wondering if he'd lost what little rational mind he had left. "Jeopardizing your kids' safety? How is letting them swim in a pool with adult supervision unsafe?"

"I was not there."

"So what? You're hardly ever here, which is why, as I understand it, you need a babysitter—me. Are you telling me then that when you're not here during the week, you're jeopardizing their safety?"

"I was not there to *protect* them." He spoke the words through his teeth as if fighting to contain some war inside of him.

Jasmine threw up her hands in frustration. "You're not here during the week to protect them. What's the difference?"

"The difference, Ms. Lewis," he said, his voice turning menacing, his expression shifting to dangerous, "is the water. The difference, Ms. Lewis, is that this family would have been devastated once again if something had happened to them—a circumstance that would have been completely *your fault* because you chose to go against my wishes for my children's safety."

He spoke as if he thought she would deliberately put his children in harm's way. Jasmine felt more than insulted. "My fault? My fault?" she started, her heart starting to sprint with agitation. "Your accusation has no foundation, *Pastor.*" Her stress on the word said she didn't think much of his title right now. "Even the Bible doesn't condemn those ignorant of sin. It's the person who knows to do right and doesn't do it that God holds responsible for the wrong. A person has to know he or she is doing something wrong in order to be held accountable for it."

"You were told!" He raised his voice at her.

Jasmine raised hers right back. "I was not! Whoever said that I knew lied."

"Why would she lie?"

So it was a female, and Jasmine immediately guessed who it was. "Scarlet Norman is a liar and a fraud," she blurted disdainfully. Her memory of the woman's fake overtures of friendship filled her with anger and revulsion.

"And isn't it interesting that you know who told me yet deny what she said? How do you know it's her if you never had a conversation about this with her?"

"Look, I don't know why she told you that lie. What I know is that she isn't a person I would trust as far as I could throw her."

"I would be careful about casting shadows on Elder Norman's character if I were you, Ms. Lewis. She's an upstanding and well respected member of my church and a true asset to my ministry. I warn you: Tread softly."

Jasmine hissed her teeth. *Upstanding my rear end.* Casting shadows? The woman's persona was enshrouded in darkness. You couldn't cast shadows over what was already murky and filthy. And who did he think he was talking to, telling her to tread softly? What if she didn't? What would he do? Jasmine might have spoken more diplomatically if he hadn't attached a threatening tone to the warning.

She strode forward, erasing the space between them. Her hands astride her hips and feet set apart, she gave full vent to her wrath. "You know what? I shouldn't expect anything better from you." She raked a scornful gaze over his frame. "You men don't have brains to think and reason things out for yourselves. It's always some woman thinking for you and leading you about by the nose or some other body part." Memories of Simon and his infidelity filtered into her mind and on into her conversation. Passion pushing her now, she warmed to her "set down" and didn't notice the change coming over

Adam King's expression—a change that didn't bode well for her, a change of a man whose injured pride demanded retribution. "If you thought for yourself, you would give me the benefit of the doubt. But you know what? Since you've passed judgment on me, I won't waste my breath and try to dissuade you. Your mind is already made up that I'm guilty. Why should I try to change your opinion? You and Scarlet Norman deserve each other. You're a cold, insensitive, and merciless man, practicing in a profession that requires the opposite. And she's a fraud, masquerading as a friendly, helpful, and kind soul. She's an asset to your ministry you say—*that* type of person," Jasmine scoffed. "Since you admire her so much, maybe you should marry her. Then you wouldn't need a babysitter." She seared him with a scathing look. "You certainly don't need me. Didn't you just say hiring me was a mistake?"

Turning sharply away, she started for the door.

Adam wasn't about to let her escape with the last word. He would teach this feisty, combative, razor-tongued woman a lesson she was unlikely to forget. He grasped her arm in a firm grip and halted her exit. He'd had numerous heart palpitations when he'd heard that she had taken the girls to the pool. What if there'd been an accident? What if one of them had been injured? What if one of them had drowned? It all would have been the fault of this careless, hardheaded, and willful female. Adam's temper intensified when he thought about it. He tugged her around and opened his mouth to give her a good dressing down.

She blasted his words back down his throat before they emerged.

"You had better take your hands off me, or so help me, I will forget that you are supposed to be a man of God, and clock you so hard, you'll never see straight again."

Adam stared at her in astonishment. The fiery intent in her eyes convinced him of her purpose. This feisty termagant, standing before him with her hands balled into fists, dared to think she could take him down! Suddenly the situation seemed so comical that Adam began to laugh.

Unamused, she leveled a malevolent stare at him. "Let me go," she ordered.

"Not a chance," he answered, moving to stand before her, still holding her arm captive. "You spoke your mind and I listened. Now you listen to me."

"I don't have to listen to you. I don't work for you anymore." Jasmine pointed out.

"You're fired when I say you are."

Jasmine hissed her teeth at that remark and tried to pry his fingers off her arm. He held that hand hostage too. "You can't do this." She glared at him.

"I just did."

Adam jumped back just before her knee disabled him. He spun her around and trapped her hands at her sides with his arms around hers. He backed up against his desk and stalled her kicking feet with his.

"This is assault, and if you value your reputation and your position, you'll let me go before I sue you."

He chuckled, truly amused by Jasmine Lewis. Since meeting her, he'd either been angry with her or amused by her, but he didn't feel indifferent and he didn't feel neutral like an employer should. What he felt for Jasmine Lewis was a mixture of emotions that were all over the place like varying volts of electricity. She made him mad, she made him smile, *and* she made him crazy. Her quick tongue and plucky attitude rubbed him wrong and arrested his attention at the same time. She wasn't trying to attract him, but she caught his interest anyway. She had an audacity and fearless boldness that made him notice her, that made him admire her, and that made him want her.

Adam had started out more than angry with her tonight. Actually he was furious. Yet by some crazy twist of emotion, his anger with her shifted to captivation with her allure—her intrepid stance and lionhearted spirit sparking the change within him. Right now he wanted her close; he wanted to touch her; and he just plain wanted her. Go figure. Like he said, she made him crazy. Holding her close like this, wanting to touch her in ways he would touch a wife, wanting to kiss her until her fighting words turned to feline purrs was insane. But there it was. That was how he felt—how she made him feel and all after making him furious. It confused his mind that she stirred two extreme emotions, anger and desire, in him in such quick succession. He pushed that mystery aside. Her petite frame fitted against his body distracted him, and his senses rose to attention at the feel of her soft parts against him. Maybe he should turn her around, but his already pounding heart might pass out from what was bound to be the blood-heating feel of her bosom against his chest. What had she said just now? That she'd sue him for assault? "Go ahead. Sue me. Your word against mine."

"You think I won't?" she asked in a tone that suggested he'd better think twice.

"According to you I can't think, I'm led around by my nose or some other body part, I believe you said, and by a woman."

Okay, Jasmine wished she hadn't said that because being close to him now, she was very aware of that unspoken body part.

"What? You have nothing to say?" he mocked gently, his breath brushing her ear like a cotton ball.

Jasmine jerked her head sideways. What was Adam King up to? "What are you doing?" she asked, wishing she sounded braver.

He kissed her earlobe and then her temple. Jasmine's heart started slamming so hard that her ribs hurt. "To tell you the truth, Jasmine, with you so near, I'm not thinking straight, so I don't really know what I'm doing." He kissed her again, this time on her cheek.

Was he going somewhere? She thought so. The path was beginning to feel like a direct trail to her lips.

"I don't think this is appropriate," she whispered, losing control of the tremor that shivered down her frame, when his lips touched the corner of her mouth.

"So what do you think I should do? Stop?"

Jasmine wasn't in a position to answer that one. Her body was craving what her mind was calling inappropriate.

"Turn around."

She obeyed the whispered command as if in a trance, knowing how this was going to end and very much wanting that end.

He slid his hands down her arms, his fingers leaving a trail of sensitivity, tantalizing pinpoints of awareness everywhere he touched. He nudged her arms away from her sides and settled his hands at her waist, his palms almost spanning it. "Petite and perfect," he murmured, watching his thumbs almost meet over her belly button.

Something sweet shifted in her chest at his admiration. "Thank you," she whispered.

He lifted his eyes from her waist and his lips curved upwards languidly, his smile a sexy parting of his mouth, revealing perfect rows of white teeth. Jasmine's knees wobbled. She clutched at his arms and held on tighter when his muscles bunched beneath her fingers, loving the feel of his strength under her hands.

He spread his feet wider to better accommodate her between his legs. With him partially seated, he didn't seem as tall. Yet Jasmine still had to look up into his face.

"You have gorgeous eyes," he complimented her. "Slanted...sexy...inviting." Jasmine's mind floated a little, each word, a low, smoky sound, dripping with seduction. "Oriental, African, beautiful."

He had pulled her closer. Jasmine knew from the gentle pressure of his hand against her back, pushing her towards his chest. She could tell too because up close like this his irises were circles of mocha brown, his pupils black buttons in the midst. He leaned in, and Jasmine closed her eyes, expecting their mouths to touch. She felt his lips brush her nose. Her eyes popped open. His gaze was low, lower than her nose, which meant he was watching her...

He touched her mouth with the tip of his finger. Jasmine kept still for a second and then trembled from the sexual sizzle of that intimate brush. He trailed his finger around the circumference of her mouth, and she couldn't stop the wobbling of her lips. His caress awakened an ache of desire in her mid-section. He cupped her chin and tipped her head up, lowering his mouth to within a breath of hers. "A work of art," he whispered against her mouth, "your lips...enticing me to taste them." And then he did it. The touch of his mouth was light, the movement of his lips felt like light brushes of air on hers, and his kisses were sweet and fleeting. Jasmine yearned for much more, and the contact promised more. The lightness of the kiss asked for patience, and the sweetness of it fueled her need for a deeper connection.

Adam gathered her closer, shifted her sideways, and tilted her over his arm. The change in her position heralded the shift in the kiss. When his lips covered hers this time, the pressure intensified the temperature of the kiss. This time she felt hunger in the length of his kiss, she felt passion in the depth of it, and desire in the urgency of it. He kissed her until she whimpered. He explored the warmth of her mouth. The erotic flicking of his tongue and its practiced placement made Jasmine heady with desire for him. Every flick, slide, glide, and stroke of his tongue was an aphrodisiac, turning embers of desire to fires of need and making her twist and moan in his arms and whisper his name like a long echo aching for an outlet that a kiss alone could not give.

When he gave them time and room to breathe, Jasmine was trembling and his breathing was far beyond ragged. He brought her slowly upright and folded her against his chest. She could feel his heart hammering as much as hers. Her thoughts tossed about like sea waves in a storm. She wasn't quite sure what happened between her attempted tempestuous exit and their sizzling encounter. But Jasmine was very sure that she wanted to be much more than Adam King's babysitter. What did he want? Why had he even kissed her? He had started out mad. What changed for him? The movement of his hands across her back distracted her from questioning him immediately. His touch felt so good, so stimulating, so awakening. His hands moved over her back, up down and all around, not following any particular pattern but just seeming content to touch her any and everywhere. He tucked his chin against her shoulder and cuddled his face close to hers. Her breasts pressed against his chest, and his hand gently urged her forward, although there was nowhere else to go. Adam King was tactile, a hugger, and a cuddler. Jasmine didn't mind. She loved that type of intimacy. She would never have guessed it of this outwardly aloof man.

"I like holding you." He admitted what she already surmised. "You feel soft, smell great, and I don't want to let go." He spanned her waist and slid his hands over the curve of her hips and then reversed the action. "You make me want things Jasmine." He didn't elaborate on the 'things' but with his gaze blazing with sexual fire, Jasmine figured it out.

"Me too," she whispered, moistening her mouth. "Maybe we shouldn't be kissing then?"

"Maybe not," he agreed and then nullified that statement by kissing her again.

"Why did you do that?" she breathed against his mouth when he eased back.

He kissed her again. "This?"

"Humm, humm."

"Because I wanted to."

"Why?"

"I could still taste you from our first kiss and I wanted more."

Jasmine kissed him now. "You don't know me. I work for you."

He chuckled against her mouth. "How are those two statements related?"

"They're not, but aren't you curious about who I am? I have so many questions that I want to ask you."

"Tell me about you."

It was an evasion. The more natural question should have been, "Like what?" But Jasmine let it go and spoke about herself. "I grew up in a home where there was love—lots of it—and I was naive enough to believe that all unions were as perfect as my parents'."

"Something shattered that belief?"

"Yes, but I don't want to talk about it." She didn't want to discuss her divorce right now. They were close and she was comfortable. Talking about divorce would put a damper on things.

"Are you an only child?" he asked, respecting her choice and changing the subject.

"Yes."

"That's why you're spoiled."

"I'm not," she contradicted, bumping her forehead against his.

"You like having your will done. You don't like criticism even the constructive kind."

"Not true. Your criticisms haven't been constructive. They've not even been criticisms."

"What then?"

"Accusations without evidence, without foundation."

"Like tonight?"

"Yes, like tonight, which makes me wonder why you don't believe that I can protect your kids at a pool when I care for them all week."

His withdrawal was immediate. He eased back, lengthening the space between their faces, and he dropped his hands from caressing her back.

Instinct guiding her, Jasmine followed him. If he laid all the way back on this table, she was going to go with him until she was laid out atop him and got the answers she sought.

"Jasmine, I don't want to talk about that," he said when he saw that he couldn't physically escape her.

"You owe me an explanation, Adam. You insulted me tonight."

He hurt her too. She would never harm his kids or let anything happen to them. For him to accuse her of being that callous injured her feelings. "I care about your kids. I would never hurt them. Why would I put them in harm's way? Do you really believe that I would have kept the girls at the pool party had I known that you didn't want them around water?"

He held her gaze for a long time before shaking his head.

Relieved, Jasmine kissed him, long, slow, and sweet, because he didn't respond at first. She felt his resistance and could tell the admission of her innocence cost him. It was as if he'd been holding onto her guilt as justification for withholding from his children an activity that they enjoyed but that he denied for reasons still unknown to her. With that excuse gone, he saw that he was hindering his kids' enjoyment of life. "On that day we had lunch in the park, I told you I'd listen if you ever needed to talk." She cradled his face and made him look at her when he tried to turn away. She kissed him. "I think you need to talk to me now, Adam."

He reached up and encircled her wrists with his hands. For a moment Jasmine thought he was going to refuse. Instead he held on tightly and closed his eyes.

"I'm afraid to let my kids near water, because Cheyenne, my wife, drowned."

Jasmine inhaled sharply. No wonder he'd been so furious earlier that she'd taken the kids to the pool. Now she understood his anger had been driven by fear of the kids falling prey to his wife's fate. She listened as he recounted the tragic experience. He hadn't wanted to go to the beach that day. He had prayed that the person they were pulling out of the water wasn't Cheyenne, but God hadn't answered his prayer. He spoke about how fragile his faith had become since then. Until recently, he still questioned why God had allowed Cheyenne to drown. But what continued to shadow his mind was the choice he made that day to yield to the pleading of his family to go to the beach. If he hadn't gone, his wife would still be alive.

Jasmine hugged him and told him that it wasn't his fault, that he couldn't control circumstances and outcomes, and that the same God he was starting to trust once again would take away his feelings of guilt. He had to let it go so that God could remove it from his mind.

Adam leaned forward and rested his forehead on her shoulder. Jasmine held him while his shoulders shook and his tears penetrated the fabric of her bolero. She kissed and soothed him, knowing that he needed the human comfort that everyone required in their time of sadness.

When he quieted, he whispered, "Thank you, Jasmine."

"I'm always here for you." She made the promise and knew she would keep it because she was in love with this man.

CHAPTER XI

Jasmine heard the low ticking of the clock on Adam's desk. She could hear their respirations. In the aftermath of his revelation, they had held each other, going on a half hour now.

"What about you?" Adam asked softly, breaking the quiet in the room. "Now you know my secret. What's yours?"

Jasmine's heart missed a beat. "I don't have one," she denied. She would have to tell him about the divorce and that other thing. She wasn't ready to share either one. Jasmine tried to turn her face away.

Adam cupped her cheek and made her meet his gaze. "That day at the park when we talked you said you had been through something that made you learn to depend on God. What was it?"

He has a good memory, Jasmine thought.

"I know you have a secret. I can see it in your tiny Asian eyes," he murmured.

"How come you never asked me about the way I look—why I look African-American and Asian at the same time?" She tried to sidetrack him. "Most people do when they see me for the first time."

He shrugged. "Who you are on the outside isn't as important as the inside."

"Clichéd answer but true."

"And you've stalled enough. You can tell me about your heritage later. I want to hear *your* secret."

"It's not really one," she began. "It's actually a matter of public record." She smiled at his quizzical look. "I'm divorced, Adam."

His whistle and raised eyebrows indicated his surprise. "Who's the stupid man that let you go?"

She laughed and kissed him. "Thank you. His name is Simon Reid. I met him eight years ago while he was studying for a master's in Public Health at Columbia."

"Columbia University in Manhattan, right?"

"Right." She sighed and laid her head on Adam's shoulder as she reflected on her marriage to Simon. "I don't know. Maybe it was his southern charm that got me or maybe it was because he was the first guy I dated. But I loved him, and for a while he treated me like there was no other woman like me."

"He made you feel special."

"Yes, he did. The strange thing was my mom never liked him. She sensed something about him wasn't quite right. She said he was too much of a flatterer, but I thought his compliments were romantic in a modern, cynical, and unromantic world. She didn't want me to marry him." She trailed a finger across the words on his T-shirt. "I should have listened to her."

"You were in love."

"Very much, so I had those blinders on. The first two years of the marriage were good. We had differences, but we worked them out. Mom even started believing that it might work, until we came to a hurdle in the marriage that we couldn't cross—well one that he couldn't cross." Jasmine pushed out of his arms. This part was much harder than admitting she was divorced.

"What hurdle was that?" Adam asked. She'd delayed too long.

She turned her back and focused on the study's door. "I can't have kids."

He didn't say anything, and Jasmine didn't look back, afraid that she might see pity or worse trepidation. Would he think that his interest was wasted on her since she was barren? If what was between them progressed to marriage, would he want a child? He already had four, but men always wanted women to have even one child for them. Didn't they? That's how Simon had been. That was the excuse he had used for his unfaithfulness. He just wanted a child. She couldn't give him one. Rhonda could. At least now he had a baby. He'd been naive enough to think she loved him so much that she would forgive his adulterous act. When she hadn't seen things his way, he'd called her some very unkind names, classifying her as a mule and saying she wasn't a full woman and her barrenness and rotten womb couldn't hold a baby.

Jasmine started when Adam's hands encased her shoulders. "I'm sorry," he said. "But you're worth far more than any baby. Simon couldn't see that. Your mother was right. He was the wrong man for you."

Jasmine turned around. Her heart started to sing when she saw none of the negative emotion she feared in his eyes. Instead she found admiration and appreciation. She slipped her hands around his waist and hugged him.

"If you don't mind my asking, why can't you have kids?"

Why was he asking that? Did it matter that she couldn't despite his encouraging words a moment ago?

"I have Polycystic Ovarian Syndrome or PCOS for short."

"What's that?" His mystified expression told that he'd never heard of it before.

"It means I have too much testosterone in my body and that causes me to ovulate and menstruate irregularly. The condition also causes insulin resistance, which prevents the endometrial lining from maturing properly."

"And if it doesn't mature, your body can't carry the pregnancy to term," he put in, understanding.

"Correct. Hence, I miscarry."

"And how many times has that happened?" His voice and expression were sympathetic now.

Jasmine turned away from it, feeling acutely impotent in the reproduction department and knowing she would cry if she kept seeing his regret on her behalf. "Ten times," she answered in a low voice. "I stopped trying after that."

"Jasmine, I'm so sorry. You'd make an amazing mom." He pulled her back into his chest and splayed his hands over her stomach. Her heart went mushy at the tender way he touched her. "In fact, you already are to my kids as I'm sure you've been to many others."

She rested her hands atop his and squeezed. "I wish Simon could have thought like you."

"I'm glad he didn't," he confessed huskily against her ear. "Otherwise you wouldn't be here now."

Jasmine laughed. "You're glad I'm divorced so you could have a babysitter for your kids? I thought you just fired me."

"Not just for the kids. Right now mostly for me."

She shifted her head sideways and looked into his face. He was serious. "You're glad I'm here?"

"Very and you're not fired. I owe you an apology. The kindness that you've shown to my children, your patience with them, and your care of them tell me that you love them. I don't know why Scarlet Norman told the story, but I no longer believe it. I shouldn't have believed it in the first place."

Jasmine knew why she had but didn't think it was the time to reveal that and break the beautiful contentment between them. "Apology accepted," she told him.

They lapsed into a comfortable silence after that. Jasmine looked at her watch. Ten thirty. He had to work tomorrow, but she didn't want to move away. He seemed pretty content to hold her too. He loosed her suddenly and threaded his fingers through hers. "Let's sit," he suggested, tugging her over to one of the armchairs by the coffee table. He sat and pulled her onto his lap.

Jasmine shifted and settled herself. She kicked off her shoes and tucked her toes into the side of the chair. Adam pulled her snugly against him and enclosed her in his arms. "You're such a tiny package."

"I'm just the right size, though. I fit right into your arms."

"I won't argue with that," he smiled.

"Can you imagine if I were as tall as you? We couldn't do this, or be like this."

"That's true. You still haven't told me about your ancestry," he reminded her, changing the topic.

"My dad was Chinese. Well he's really Jamaican but his forefathers came from China."

"Sounds like interesting history."

"It is. When slavery was abolished in Jamaica, the plantation owners brought in what they called 'indentured laborers' to work the sugar plantations. These laborers came from India and China. My father was a direct descendant of Chinese indentured laborers."

"How come your name is so English? I would have thought it would be Chin, Chung, Yee, Lee or something like that."

My grandmother, my dad's mom, remarried when her Chinese husband died. Her second husband was black. His name was Lewis and he adopted my dad."

"I see. You speak of your father in the past tense. I take it he died."

She nodded.

"And your mother, where is she from?"

"From New York and she's African-American. What about your family?"

"Do you want to know where they're from?"

"Yes and anything else you want to tell me about them."

"My parents are native Floridians. They came to New York as newlyweds to look for better economic opportunities. They worked and raised a family in Queens. My dad died from a pulmonary embolism just before he retired. My mother remarried and retired to Florida with my step-father. I have two brothers and two sisters. I'm the only one still braving the New York cold. My sister, Gilene, lives in St. Thomas, U.S. Virgin Islands with her family. My brother, Seth is in South Carolina. Blair lives in London with his wife, and Tamara lives in Florida near my mother."

"Are you the oldest child?"

"No, the second. Seth is older than I am."

"He doesn't have family?" She noticed Adam hadn't mentioned that he had.

He shook his head. "He never married. I'm not sure he ever will. He's set in his ways. I'm not sure any woman will tolerate his taciturn disposition and mulish ways."

"You'd be surprised. My dad always used to say every stick has its half a hoe in the bush."

Adam grinned. "Translate that for me."

"Everybody has somebody who will love them."

He gave her a strange smile, and Jasmine wondered what he was thinking. She cuddled closer. This was cozy. She didn't want to move, but tomorrow was a work day and Adam especially had to rest. "We should say good night," she said reluctantly.

"We should," he agreed but didn't move.

"You have to work tomorrow, Adam. You should go to bed."

"The chair reclines," he pointed out. "We could sleep here."

Somehow the suggestion held more appeal than scandal. She remembered the children. "What would the children think if they found us like this in the morning?"

"They don't usually come in here, but I think they'd approve if they did."

The girls had certainly intimated that, but she wasn't sure about the boys. She asked him.

"Funny you should ask," Adam said. "Adam, Jr. and I talked earlier and he asked me, kind of sly-like if I noticed your beauty. I wondered why he asked that. He said he wouldn't mind if I did notice. So I don't think they'd mind if they found us together."

It was good to know they had the kids' approval, but approval for what? Chemistry for sure choked the air every time they got close. Without a doubt they liked each other. But where did they want to take this interest they had in each other? Not marriage? Jasmine hadn't thought about it since her divorce, but now that she'd met Adam King, the idea held appeal. What were his thoughts? She would have to remain in the dark. She wasn't about to ask him if he wanted to marry her. She was bold but not that much.

Tipping her head back, Jasmine puckered her lips for a kiss. "One for the road," she requested.

Adam complied and gave her several that had him helping her up the stairs to her room afterwards.

CHAPTER XII

On the following Wednesday and all during prayer meeting, Scarlet Norman sensed Pastor King's distance towards her. Had Jasmine contradicted her lie, and did he believe Jasmine? Scarlet knew she would have done the same had the roles been reversed. Now Adam was keeping her at arms' length. She was guilty of lying, but that was immaterial to Scarlet. What was important was getting Adam to be comfortable around her again and getting him to trust her. At the end of service, Scarlet took immediate steps to restore her place in Adam's good graces.

She waited until he finished talking to parishioners and followed him into his study. She started with a familiar opening line. "Sis. James didn't come to service tonight."

He glanced over his shoulder and replied, "Thanks. I know."

Abrupt, to the point, and no frills. *Wow. She was fully in the dog house.* Usually, he'd smile and murmur an appreciation for her attention to detail. Not so this time. In fact he'd stated the 'I know' as if impatient with her for stating the obvious. It was way past time to breach the growing chasm.

"Pastor King, may I speak with you?"

His bag in hand he turned to her. The smile he sent her way had none of his usual ease and warmth. It came and left faster than the bat of her eyelash. "Sure, Elder. What's on your mind?"

He didn't say her name like he always did. Just 'Elder' he'd called her—impersonal and cold.

Scarlet decided to give the performance of her life. She linked her fingers before her, consciously twisting them as if she were distressed. "I shared some information with you on Sunday and have been regretting it ever since."

His right eyebrow inched upwards. Good. She had his attention. "I never should have shared that information about what Jasmine did on Sunday," she blurted in a rush, as if it were a burden she couldn't wait to unload.

He looked taken aback. "And why is that?" he asked.

"She's your employee, and I hope I didn't jeopardize her job." Crying had always come easy to Scarlet. She could turn it on and off like the shower. Right now she turned it on, and tears sprang and flooded her eyes. Through a shimmer of moisture, she saw the shift in his face from stern to sympathetic. Waterworks never fail, she gloated in silent triumph.

In a soothing, gentle voice, he said, "Please don't distress, yourself, Elder. Ms. Lewis's job is safe."

"I'm glad." She smiled big, mimicking huge relief and brushing crocodile tears from the corners of her eyes.

He studied her thoughtfully, opened his mouth and then closed it as if he thought better of it.

"What is it?" Scarlet prompted him.

He didn't answer immediately. He searched her expression for a while and finally said, "Jasmine maintains she didn't know I didn't want my kids at the pool."

Scarlet stepped back, her expression perfectly outlining shock. "But I told her," she protested.

"She says you didn't."

"Why would she say that?" Scarlet pulled bewilderment and hurt out of her theatrical hat.

He shrugged.

"Maybe she misunderstood me?" she offered.

His raised brow broadcasted skepticism. *He believes her.* Scarlet chose to end it, save face, and hoped to retain Adam's respect. "Whatever the case, please know it wasn't my intent to cause trouble. I'm truly sorry if I did." She turned the tears back on. "Please tell Jasmine that for me," she sniffed and walked off.

Two paces away, his voice stopped her, and his words made her smile.

"I'll tell her, Elder. And stop worrying. I know you didn't mean any harm."

Hiding her satisfaction behind another sniffle, she turned to him. "Thanks, Pastor. It means a lot to hear that."

His genuine smile was back in place and his expression was once again warm and friendly. Great, she thought. I'm back in his circle.

Good night, Elder Norman. By God's grace I'll see you on Sabbath."

"Good night Pastor. Get home safely."

As she sailed out the door, Scarlet thought that it was time to put plan B in place. Plan A—the pool party lie had failed.

CHAPTER XIII

Three Weeks Later

"I beg your pardon." Adam cocked his head, not sure he'd heard his boss correctly.

Anthony Stubbs, president of the conference of churches in which Adam worked, regarded him seriously. "Pastor, three of your parishioners have called with the same concern. I thought it prudent to speak with you in person about the allegation and to hear your response to it."

Adam didn't know Anthony Stubbs well, not like he had known his predecessor Jeremiah Brown. If Jeremiah had been the president, he'd never have summoned him with the preposterous claim that he was living in sin with a woman who was not his wife. Jeremiah knew him well and knew he wouldn't do something like that. Anthony Stubbs didn't know him. Adam swallowed his anger at the outrageous accusation the man had just laid out and focused on formulating a calm answer. He wished he knew who the parishioners were, but Stubbs wouldn't reveal that. He couldn't think of anyone who would spread a lie like that.

"Jasmine Lewis is babysitter for my children," he explained. "She lives in my house—true. But that's an arrangement that enables her to do her job more effectively and it is economically beneficial to both of us."

President Stubbs raised his eyebrows but merely said, "Go on."

Adam didn't have anything more to add and wondered why the

man expected more. "That's about it President Stubbs. Ms. Lewis and I aren't having an affair. She works for me. That's all."

Anthony Stubbs leaned forward and placed his elbows on the massive cherry wood desk separating him from Adam. He propped up his chin on his fists and studied Adam thoughtfully. "In first Thessalonians five, twenty-two, the word of God warns us to abstain from evil. Wait a minute." He raised his hand as Adam opened his mouth to protest. "I'm not saying you're indulging in evil. However, you are a single man; and this young lady, as I understand it, isn't married. To the outsider, your circumstances may appear clandestine, although it is innocent."

Adam ground his teeth in annoyance. "My single state is the very reason I hired Ms. Lewis. I'm gone a lot and early. There's no one to help my kids get ready for school, get the younger ones on the bus, help with homework and cook for them. She does it because I can't."

Stubbs sighed. "I understand your situation and also your frustration Pastor King, but we can't have your character compromised or your image tarnished in the eyes of the membership. It's not good for you, it's not good for the ministry, and it retards the promulgation of the gospel."

"What retards the promulgation of the gospel is wagging, unbridled tongues spreading lies about my relationship with Jasmine Lewis," Adam gritted.

The president inclined his head in agreement. "While that is true," he said, "three members have voiced their concern about the young lady living in your house. We don't want them to spread their discontent to the other members, so we must take steps to rectify the situation."

"Rectify the situation?" Adam didn't like the sound of that.

"Yes, Ms. Lewis needs to leave your place of residence."

Adam didn't respond right then. If he had, he would have lost his job. With supreme effort, he managed to make his voice sound reasonable. "Earlier I said that the living arrangement was economically beneficial to both of us. With her living in my house, she's readily available to the kids, but it also saves me from paying her an extra five hundred dollars a month. If she moves out, I'll have to come up with that money, and right now, Pastor Stubbs, I don't have that extra cash. Also, she's saving on rent. The apartment she had was costing her eight hundred a month plus food. Her room and board are included in our arrangement."

"I see the practicality of all you are saying, Pastor King, but the profession you practice requires moral integrity. Ms. Lewis living in your home compromises that integrity."

The president's stubborn expression communicated that he was not open to discussion. Adam could see that there would be no negotiating him out of his decision. Still he asked, "What do you suggest I do then?"

"Ms. Lewis will have to move out."

"If she moves out, I'll not be able to pay her and hence will be unable to keep her services."

"If she doesn't, we won't be able to keep *your* services."

Adam went very still. He'd be terminated the man meant. He'd heard that the guy could be hard and unsympathetic. Now he believed it. "I see," he said quietly. Resting his hands on his knees, he prepared to get up and get out. "If there's nothing further President Stubbs, I'll let myself out."

"Just one more thing," the man said, rising from his chair with an amiable smile, now that Adam had gotten his message loud and clear. "You have two weeks to correct this situation."

Adam didn't bother to protest that it wasn't enough time. He rose, picked up his briefcase, and with a clipped, "Good afternoon, sir," to his boss, he exited the office.

CHAPTER XIV

Adam remembered he'd told Jasmine he'd bring dinner and she wasn't to cook tonight. He planned to stop at Selena's, a Mexican-American restaurant in Mountain Spring and pick up some take out. His thoughts tumbling from his meeting with the president, he remembered his promise just as he passed the Mountain Spring exit. He turned around and got off the highway on the opposite side.

His phone rang as he pulled into Selena's parking. "Hi, Jasmine," he answered.

"Adam, we have a problem."

You have no idea. "What's the matter?"

"Do you remember the rushing sound of water we've been hearing in the walls all week?"

"Yes."

"Well, I found the cause of it."

"What's that?"

"It looks like there's a busted pipe at the left side of the house because water is bubbling up from underground. The ground is completely saturated."

Adam closed his eyes and rested his head against the head rest. Great. More money that he didn't have. "Do me a favor. Look on the fridge and you'll see a magnet advertising Haynes Plumbing. Call the number and ask for Solomon. Tell him the problem, and he'll send someone out to fix it."

"I'll do that," she promised and then added. "Are you all right? You sound weary."

Adam smiled a little. "I'm a bit tired," he admitted. Jasmine was very perceptive. He'd noticed it these past weeks. He liked corn bread baked with kernels of corn. She made it once, and he practically ate the whole pan. After that she never made it without putting the kernels in. He kept forgetting to remove the stiffening from his shirt collars before taking them to the cleaners and kept losing them to the cleaning process. When he came downstairs in the morning without stiffening, she always produced some. Adam found out she'd been removing the stiffening from his soiled shirts. He liked the attention and the care that she gave. He was paying her to take care of the kids. Taking care of him was extra, which meant it was something she did because she wanted to and not because she had to. It made Adam feel special.

Things had shifted between them since she took the girls to the pool party and he'd confronted her. Since that disagreement and the subsequent make-up, they'd grown close and become more comfortable around one another. They spoke easily, laughed much, and they had a friendship. She'd started making him breakfast and packing him a lunch. At first he'd protested, but within two days he had shut up and counted his blessings. Dinner came next. It was nice not only to walk in to a hot meal but to be served one as well. Jasmine had taken to doing that. He hadn't protested about that, liking it too much and even more the fact that she stayed and talked to him while he ate.

Adam found that she occupied his thoughts more and more while he drove and filtered into his dreams at night. He hardly thought about Cheyenne these days and the piercing pain of her loss had dulled to barely an ache. He thought he'd feel like a betrayer, but he didn't. Adam realized he accepted her absence and was ready to move on with his life and with a new love.

His breath pushed out in short puffs. Was this feeling of contentment he experienced around Jasmine love? Was his eagerness to get home at night the same thing? This time it had come differently. With Cheyenne it had been passionate, urgent, and involved lots of feelings. With Jasmine, the awareness was there, the desire present without a doubt, but there was companionship and an eagerness to rush home every night. Her presence made his house a home again. She had healed his heart.

Lost in his thoughts as he walked into Selena's, he startled when someone touched his shoulder.

"Pastor King."

Adam looked up to face the smiling countenance of Solomon Haynes. The tall, fair-skinned man was a few inches above Adam's six feet five. "Bro. Haynes," he greeted the plumber with a smile. "I was just talking about you."

"Really?"

"Yes. I've got a busted pipe at the side of my house. I wonder if you could take a look at it." Adam had had some plumbing work done on the house when he'd initially bought it. Solomon Haynes had done the work and a good job too. He'd kept the man's contact.

"I'll come by tomorrow between nine and ten to take a look at it. Just call my office and leave your address with my secretary."

"Okay, I'll d—"

"Daddy, daddy, over here."

Adam followed the line of Solomon's gaze and turned around to see a short woman in an advanced state of pregnancy approaching them with two large department store bags in either hand. A girl was walking with her and trying to take the bags from her.

"My wife," Solomon muttered on a sigh. "She's so stubborn." He strode over to them and firmly removed the bags from his wife's hand. Adam watched in amusement as the woman rolled her eyes while the girl grinned.

"Pastor King," Solomon said when the three of them got to Adam, "Please meet my wife, Grace, who refuses to admit that she needs help even in her eighth month of pregnancy."

The woman laughed and shook Adam's hand. "Hello, Pastor," she said. "And my husband just refuses to admit that pregnancy doesn't curb independence."

Solomon rolled his eyes now, but the look he sent towards his wife was filled with love and tolerance.

"Hi, Pastor King. I'm Rebecca," the girl, who was a replica of her mother introduced herself since her father had failed to do that. "And I'm going to have a brother in a month. I get to name him, and I'm calling him Seth."

Adam shook the hand of the precocious young girl with the sweet smile and silver braces. "I'm happy for you, and I think Seth will be very glad for a sister who's so excited about him. I have a brother named Seth. It's a good name."

She grinned wider.

"Until tomorrow, Solomon. It was nice meeting you Sis. Haynes.

Bye, Rebecca." Adam waved goodbye and headed into Selena's.

***

Something was troubling Adam. They'd had a family dinner with the take out from Selena's. The kids had gone upstairs, and they were alone. She had baked a cake, but Adam hadn't touched the slice she had given him. He had barely eaten his dinner.

Jasmine got up and scooted her chair closer to his. She reached out and took the cake from him and set it on the coffee table. "What's bothering you, Adam?" she asked, getting straight to the point.

He shifted and stretched his long legs out before him. "If I said nothing you wouldn't believe me, would you?"

"You know I wouldn't. You hardly ate any dinner, and you're not eating the cake I labored to make just for you."

"Thanks, but I'm just not hungry tonight."

"You're hungry every night, so what's the problem?" She touched his brow. "You don't have fever, so you're not sick. What cut your appetite?"

"I had a very disturbing conversation with the conference president earlier today."

"Disturbing how?"

Adam heard the frown in her voice. Her brows were creased when he looked at her. He smoothed them. "Don't do that. It will put lines on your beautiful face."

She smiled at his admission of her beauty.

His stomach fluttered. He stretched out his hand, palm up. She placed her hand in his and he threaded their fingers together.

"He thinks we're living together as more than babysitter and employer."

"What! Where did he get that from?"

"Somebody, well some people—three, according to him—called the conference to complain about my distasteful domestic situation."

Jasmine's small hand had a firm grip. Adam felt the power in it as anger made her tighten her hold on him.

Jasmine felt her pressure keep pace with her temper. Three people? The first would be Scarlet Norman. The next was probably Gretta and the other could be any one of those forgeries of genuine humanity from the pool party a few weeks back. She spoke her thoughts because she needed an outlet for some of her internal aggravation. "Scarlet Norman is involved in this."

"You don't know that, Jasmine," Adam cautioned.

She snatched her hand from his. "Why are you so blind? The woman told a whopping lie once, and you still believe she's a saint?"

"Jasmine, everybody makes mistakes."

"Oh." She drew back and leveled a look full of frustration at him. "So her lie is a mistake now?"

"She apologized and said she didn't mean to cause trouble."

"She apologized to you, not to me whom she wronged. And she never admitted that she lied; so the apology was meaningless when she didn't own up to her wrong doing."

"What motive would she have for telling the conference president that we're living in sin, Jasmine?"

Jasmine looked to the ceiling and debated about telling him what she'd overheard at the pool party. "She wants you."

"Me?" Adam looked confused.

"I overheard a conversation between her and some of her friends at the pool party. She wants me out of this house and out of the picture because she wants you for herself."

"That doesn't make sense. I have no interest in her, and she's never expressed an interest in me."

"That's because she's slick and sly. From the number of times she calls you at night and on the weekends, I'd have known she was interested even without overhearing her admit it."

"Her calls are always church related." He frowned. "You actually heard her express an interest in me?"

"I did. Remember when we argued after the pool party, you said she was an asset to you and to your ministry?"

He nodded.

"I suspect that she's made herself that way so that you can appreciate her value. Maybe she's hoping you'll see beyond her church value to a more personal one."

"I'm finding this very hard to believe."

Jasmine could understand that the perfect image he had of the woman was a little difficult to shake. She went back to his meeting with the president. "So what else did the president say? Are you being suspended? Are you on probation?"

"You have to move out."

"And if I don't?"

"I'll be terminated."

Jasmine went to the window. She looked out, the beauty of the full moon not registering with the agitation inside her. "You know, this would not have been a problem had I been your mother's age."

"I know."

"What's getting me irritated is that we're not guilty of anything, so what's the problem?" She turned to face him.

"According to the president, we need to shun the 'appearance' of evil, so that I can maintain my 'moral integrity'—his words."

"If there's anyone immoral in this it's the people who called the conference and lied." She wanted to say Scarlet Norman but knew he wasn't quite a believer in the woman's guilt. Jasmine turned back to the window when he didn't say anything.

"I'll start looking for a place," she spoke into the lengthy silence behind her.

"There's an alternative."

Jasmine jerked at the sudden sound of his voice behind her. She glanced over her shoulder. "What alternative is that?"

He reached down and took her hand. "Walk with me outside. I want to talk to you."

"About what?" Jasmine tipped her head up and searched his eyes, but he gave nothing away.

"About the alternative," he said, his tone more mysterious than his words.

Jasmine allowed him to tug her outdoors. He slipped an arm around her shoulders and she curved her hand about his waist. He shortened his stride to match hers. The night was quiet. The sky glistened from the half moon's glow, and the trees and hedges formed background shadows, their fringes sparkling like silver where the moonlight kissed the leaves. It was warm not hot. Being close wasn't a problem. It was semi-dark not pitch black—shadowy enough for secret kisses; not dark enough for trouble. Romance rode on the air. With Adam this close and with the elusive scent of his cologne seeping into her senses, it felt like a date with a man who mattered. And Adam King had come to matter more than Jasmine felt comfortable admitting.

"The first time I saw you," Adam began, "you floored me, and then you aggravated me. Last of all you intrigued me." He glanced down at her with a quick smile. "I'm still interested."

Jasmine chuckled. "You annoyed me first and then caught my eye against my will."

"There have been times when I wanted to strangle you."

"Times where you wanted to fire me," Jasmine added.

"Yes, quite a few of those," he said dryly.

"But most of all you wanted to hug and coddle me," Jasmine said with a cheeky grin.

"That's the baffling part. You upset me one minute and I wish you were in another country. The next moment I want to embrace you and keep you close."

"That's the mystery of me," Jasmine laughed.

"You have a sassy tongue, you know that?"

"Come on, Adam, I'm just honest."

"I like that about you. I also like the fact that you're courageous and bold. There are no shades of grey with you. You've got a refreshing and engaging personality."

"Oh, Adam, I think that's the nicest thing you've ever said to me. Thank you." She squeezed his waist.

He stepped off the paved driveway and unto the grass. Stopping beneath a wide-trunked maple, he leaned against it. When he tugged her between his widened feet, Jasmine went willingly and rested against his chest.

"What I admire most about you though, is the way you are with my kids."

"The way I am?" Jasmine raised a brow.

"You treat them like they're your own."

"I love kids, Adam."

"I know, but you love my kids."

"How do you know that I'm not just doing my job?"

"Technically, your job ends on Friday around three o'clock. Why then do the girls spend every Saturday night for the past three weekends in your room when you're off the clock?"

Jasmine pushed off his chest surprised. "You know about that?"

"Yeah I know. When my kids are not in their beds I know. I asked them. They told me they have an appointment with you to watch movies and eat snacks late into the night and into the early hours of Sunday morning."

"I hope you don't mind. I think I enjoy it more than they do. I look forward to it."

"That's what I'm talking about. You love it. That's why you do it. You love my kids, and I'm thankful for that. I feel blessed."

Jasmine saw the gratitude in his eyes and tears burned hers because he had no idea how much it meant to her to be a part of something she could never have. To act as a mother to children she would never bear and to enjoy things with Dona and Claire that girls did with their moms were privileges. The appreciation was hers. He couldn't begin to understand unless their roles were reversed. "Thank you, Adam, for sharing your children with me. I'm the one who's blessed."

He pulled her closer and cupped her cheek. "There's one more thing I want to share with you."

He meant a kiss, Jasmine thought, as her eyes focused to his mouth. His head drifted closer, and she turned hers up in anticipation. She closed her eyes as he lowered his head. Their breath intermingled and Jasmine sighed, longing riding out on that puff of air.

"My heart," he whispered.

Jasmine's eyes flew wide. *His heart?* "Wha-what?" she stuttered.

"I love you, Jasmine. Will you marry me?"

Jasmine pushed out of his embrace. Two emotions swapped places in rapid succession in her heart, confusing that organ and making it thunder. Explosive happiness danced with bone deep fear. Another man had declared love once but it hadn't lasted. He hadn't known she was barren at the time of the declaration. Her reproductive inability had killed that love. But Adam knew, and he still loved her. But suppose he wanted more children later on and changed his mind about the 'til-death-do-us-part' commitment? Would he change his mind? Could she trust that love to last?

"Jasmine what is it?" His question was uncertain and his voice a little hurt. She understood that she hadn't returned his affection by word or deed. He brushed his thumb across her cheek, wiping away tears that she was only now beginning to feel. "I'd hoped you loved me too. I had no idea that my love would hurt you." His words were strained and his expression was filled with sadness.

Jasmine wiped her eyes and swallowed the lump in her throat. "I love you too, Adam. I'm just not sure how long you will love me."

"I don't understand."

"I can't give you children, Adam."

Understanding swamped his face and relief too. He took her hands in his. "Jasmine I have four kids. I don't want any more."

"But suppose you change your mind later?"

He ignored the question. "What I want is you, Jasmine."

"Despite the fact that I'm broken?" she whispered.

He tugged her back into his embrace. "You are not broken," he said firmly. "You are perfect."

She snuggled closer. "Say that again," she mumbled against his chest."

"You're not broken."

"The other part."

"You're perfect." He kissed her and repeated it until she believed it.

When she ran out of air and waved her white flag with the words "I believe you," Adam gave her rest.

"You didn't answer my question," he reminded her.

"What was it again?" Jasmine asked, her mind still drifting in the afterglow of his kiss.

"Will you marry me, Jasmine Lewis?"

She nodded.

"Say it," he commanded.

"Yes, I'll marry you."

He kissed her with the strength of joy her reply created within him.

When she could breathe again she asked, "What about the kids? Do you think they'll be okay with this?"

"More than okay."

"Did they tell you that?" she asked worriedly.

"They like the idea of having a mother again and know that with marriage you'll be theirs officially, so, yes, they are on board."

Jasmine laughed in relief, and then she asked as she remembered. "Was this the alternative you spoke about earlier?"

"It is, although now I don't think of it as an alternative. It's more like the sole solution. Your moving out was never an option. I wouldn't have let you leave me."

"But you would have lost your job."

"Only if you had turned me down," he grinned. "Because then I would have made you stay and made their lie about us living in sin the truth."

"Oh, Adam, you're crazy and I love you."

"I love you too, Jasmine, very much."

She placed her hand against his cheek. "You know, my job offer being rescinded seemed like a disaster at the time. Meeting you and falling for you tell me that God allowed that as a stepping stone to your love and a ready-made family."

"All things work together for the good of God's children—the good and bad things." As he said the words, Adam realized they applied to him too. He'd lost a good woman. God had filled that void with a great one.

EPILOGUE

Jasmine had been a bride for just twenty-four hours, and one night in Adam's arms had left her craving for many more. They had married yesterday at the courthouse with their mothers as witnesses while the children looked on. It was now Sabbath. They had delayed their honeymoon so Adam could inform his church of his newly wedded state and let them know he'd be away for two Sabbaths. Their mothers would watch the kids while they were gone.

Adam had finished preaching, and the closing song had been sung. He asked the congregation to sit for a moment of meditation and information.

"My brothers and sisters," he started. "The Bible tells us that every good and perfect gift comes from above. Well for the past two months I've been experiencing one of God's gifts and just yesterday, that gift got icing on the cake so to speak."

A murmur of curiosity ran through the congregation. Members glanced at each other with clueless looks. Jasmine suppressed a smile and elbowed Claire in the side when the girl giggled.

"The gift I'm speaking of is none other than my wife, Jasmine King."

The hush that fell over the sanctuary was complete. Were the members shocked, dismayed, or joyful? Jasmine didn't glance around to find out, even though she itched to.

"Jasmine, sweetheart, can you come up here please?"

He hadn't told her he was going to do this, but Jasmine rose from her seat, slipped past her children and out the pew. She felt like every eye in the congregation was on her, but she kept her head high and looked straight ahead at the man who was smiling at her, love pouring from him and giving her the strength to keep walking. She was almost at the podium where Adam stood when a loud whistle rent the air, and the voice of her son, Drew, who hardly spoke, shattered the quiet. "Yes! That's my mom," he yelled and started clapping. By the time she finished the four steps that took her to her husband's side, the entire congregation was on its feet and applauding...except one person.

Jasmine wasn't sure if anybody else noticed, but she saw Scarlet Norman slink out a side exit, and she could have sworn the woman brushed a tear away from her cheek.

***

"Leaving already, Scarlet? Don't you want to give your well wishes to the pastor and his new wife?"

Scarlet whirled at the sound of Gretta's goading voice. "Shut up, Gretta! Just shut up!"

Gretta pulled a hurt look. "Is that any way to treat the friend who helped you lie to the president to get Jasmine out of Adam King's house?"

The noise that came from somewhere low in Scarlet's throat had the guttural growl of a grizzly.

"Oh, but I forgot," Gretta went on with feigned sympathy. "That didn't work did it? Instead of getting out of his house, Jasmine ended up in his bed as his wife. And it's all thanks to your ingenuity."

"I hate you! You were the one who told me to call the conference president!" Scarlet screamed, before dragging open the door of her Jaguar, and flinging herself into the driver's seat.

Gretta watched her race out of the parking lot as if committed to killing herself. She walked back into the church, thinking women needed to wake up and realize no man was worth wasting that kind of emotion over.

***

Nine months later

Jasmine watched the Minivan race down the driveway with her husband and maternity bag while she stood on the porch and shook her head. Hopefully he would realize his passenger was missing before he got to the hospital. She leaned against one of the columns next to the front door and breathed by counts as another contraction hit. She heard the scream of brakes being applied hard. He was back within a minute. He flew out of the jeep and rushed towards her.

"Babe, I thought you were in the car," he said shakily. The hand he placed beneath her elbow trembled too. Jasmine wondered if she should wake up Adam, Jr. to do the driving. She gripped her husband's arm and made it to the van.

Jasmine whimpered as a contraction hit.

"Are you all right?" he asked anxiously.

"I'm fine," she managed. That contraction had been severe.

He stepped on the gas harder.

This baby was a miracle child. The fact that she had carried it to term without a miscarriage was an act of God. It was a girl, and she and Adam agreed that their daughter could have no other name than Miracle. And with the last three contractions coming two minutes apart, it would be a miracle if they made it to the hospital in time.

But make it they did, and for the next four hours Jasmine endured what had to be the most excruciating pain on the face of the earth as she labored to bring her daughter into the world. Miracle put in an appearance at six a.m. and screamed like she was supposed to, only shutting up when they put her to her mother's breast.

Three hours later, a refreshed but still worn looking Adam returned with the children and each one took their time admiring their sister. Daniel thought she looked wrinkled. Claire and Dona, of course, took up for their gender and considered her Ms. Universe. Adam, Jr. made no comment, but his smile said he was proud of his sister.

While their children admired the new addition to the family, Adam pulled up a chair next to his wife's bedside.

"How are you feeling, babe?"

"Exhausted and happy."

"Sore and achy?"

"That too but mostly happy."

"And thankful?"

"Lots of that."

"God is good," Adam said.

"He's better. He's great."

"Amen."

With that he leaned in and kissed his wife gently on the lips, thanking God quietly for her and for their Miracle.

THE END

Upcoming Titles

A Matter of Trust
(Seneca Mountain Romances: Book 4)
<u>Coming July 2014</u>

Adrianna, Dri, wants to start a family. Her husband, Christopher, does too. Sounds like they're on the same page? Not quite. Haunted by an old tragedy, he wants to adopt. Dri wants to do things the traditional way. Christopher can't bring himself to give her what she wants. Reason, ranting, and rivers of tears don't change his mind. Dri hatches a private plan and secures his unwitting cooperation. But she doesn't remember that her condition can't be camouflaged forever. When her husband finds out what she has done, he is livid. With the trust between them torn down, Dri realizes too late that she got what she wanted at the expense of what she needs—her husband and his trust.

Not His Choice
(Five Brothers Books: Book 4)
<u>Coming May 2014</u>

If you've been following the five brothers, you already met James (From Passion to Pleasure), John (Once in This Lifetime), and Nate (Someone Like You). Here's a summary of **Peter's** *story in* **Not His Choice:**

Peter Roach is a bachelor and loving it. Three of his four brothers have taken well to wedded bliss. Peter's desire is polar opposite. When a woman, who doesn't fit the 'in-need' bill, walks into Carla's Soup Kitchen, Peter reluctantly helps her as tears start to fall. One argument; one offer of a ride; and one offer of accommodation get him involved in Pamela Brinkley's life deeper than the meaning of the word. The funny thing is, after just a few days of knowing her, the single life is starting to lose a lot of luster.

Pamela Brinkley is a single mother, raising her four kids. Her salary seems to shrink monthly. There's always a cash flow problem—money floods out of her bank account. The man who saves her from being stranded by giving her a ride when her car breaks down gives her shelter the same night when her oil runs out. Peter Roach is an incredible human being. Pamela is baffled that he continues to stick around after his Good Samaritan acts. Not many modern men would do all that for a girl with four kids. One hot kiss on a stormy night reminds her that she has needs she's been neglecting. Stick around, Peter!

A heart ache from the past reminds Peter why he should steer clear of heart entanglement in the present. With Pamela and her situation so similar to Marianne and hers, can Peter trust that Pam won't break his heart? The trouble is that Pamela may be forced to make a choice that will cost her the love of the man she cares for—Peter Roach.

Local Gold
(Five Brothers Books: Book 5)
1ˢᵗ James, 2ⁿᵈ John, 3ʳᵈ Nate, 4ᵗʰ Peter, and now here's **Bart**
<u>Coming June 2014</u>

Brianna and Bart have been dancing around each other for years. A bad relationship and a baby made her commit to a man-free life. So what's this that she's feeling for Bart? He's been a friend for too long, yet more and more her feelings towards him are anything but filial.

He fell for her from the time he met her heartbroken and pregnant. He offered friendship because that was what she needed at the time. But with her son, whom he claims as his own, calling him father—he's the only dad the child knows—and with them sharing a house, this feels like the real deal which is a wife and family. Tired of settling for the counterfeit, Bart wants the real thing. He's waited too long—six years and going—for Bri's love. He decides to take a shot at losing his heart or gaining her love. Will she reject or receive him?

Emeralds Aren't Forever
(The Banning Island Romances: Book 3)
<u>Coming Fall 2014</u>

On a Spanish American Cruise vacation, Sarah has no idea how valuable the stone on her purse's clasp is. When she nearly gets mugged in Cartagena and almost thrown overboard later, she solicits help from the man who saved her both times—Everton Marsh. An ex-revolutionary and a sometimes security specialist, Everton had wanted a peaceful vacation. This American woman, Sarah, wasn't letting that happen. Together, they uncover a ring of emerald thieves, stretching from Cartagena to New York and to all parts of the Caribbean. Danger rises for Sarah as these thieves are willing to murder whoever blocks them from the emeralds. Now more than ever she needs Everton's protection. After one slow dance on a dark deck one night, Sarah realizes that she wants more than his protection.

Existing Titles

A Fall for Grace
(Seneca Mountain Romances: Book 1)
<u>Excerpt</u>

"How are you, Grace? It's been a long time."

Fury shot a swift path from her brain to her mouth, and Grace forgot all her careful effort these past twelve years to never let passion dominate her person again. "*Now* you want to know how I am?! *Now*, after twelve years, you have the audacity to ask me that!!! How dare you?! How dare you?! You worthless excuse for a man." Grace remembered in the nick of time that she had a child in the house that she didn't want to hear this tirade. She lowered her voice, but the venom in her came across loudly and clearly. "You took what I had to give and left me without a backward glance, never responding to my SOS calls about the pregnancy. You appeased a need, scratched an itch with a stupid, innocent girl and left me to bear the disgrace of it. What kind of callous, despicable, disgusting person are you? 'It's been a long time' you say so casually. Yes, it *has* been a long time—a long time since you made my life a living hell!" Grace paused and scrubbed shaking hands over her face, fighting for control. Good God she wanted to hit him, pummel him, hurt him the way he'd hurt her. Reaching deeply for composure, she found enough to say, "Just fix my toilet and boiler and get out." With that she turned and walked away, every step forced, screaming in protest with the still bottled anger that needed the convenient outlet behind her—Solomon Haynes.

A Price Too High
(Seneca Mountain Romances: Book 2)
<u>Excerpt</u>

Karen stared and slowly began to realize just what he was thinking. Oh, dear, father. He thought she had slept with someone else! Anger chased close to the heels of that awareness. Before she could catch the words, they escaped. "How dare you! I'm not that sort of woman. How can you think that I would sleep with someone else?"

"*Don't* raise your voice at me." His response was low, quiet, but very dangerous—the force of the words making them so.

"Well, don't accuse me of something so unsavory. I'm not a slut!"

"I didn't accuse you of anything, and I don't know what you really are except that you are an accomplished and pathological liar!"

Karen could not deny outright the liar part so she said, "If you don't want me to raise my voice, don't raise yours."

"Last I checked, the lease to this place was in my name. I'll do and say as I please and anyhow I please." His gaze raked her from crown to toes and backwards, his look withering and dismissive. "Now, why don't you tell me why you came to me after seven months?"

Confession time. Karen bit her lip and then bit the bullet. "I lost my job and my apartment. I had nowhere else to go."

Silence clapped like thunder and then sat like a weight in the room.

She watched him close his eyes, and press his fingers against his eyelids. Karen didn't know what that meant.

Once in This Lifetime
(Five Brothers: Book 2)
<u>Excerpt</u>

"Excuse me, miss. Did you happen to notice a young woman sitting at the table ahead of you a few moments ago?"

The voice was gentle, quiet, like the words issued forth effortlessly yet with a depth of sound that was thunder and caress at the same time. Julia shivered, the sound of that voice sliding down her spine like silk over skin. Tilting her head back, way back, she looked a long way up and her gaze got kidnapped by the bluest, most brilliant eyes she'd ever beheld. He wasn't a brother after all—at least not a black brother. That realization was quickly followed by awareness that he was an attractive man. Well, without the blue eyes he was attractive; with them he was arresting. He was blond, with hair low cut like a military man. His thick eyebrows were straight, nearly meeting above the bridge of his long, narrow nose, the rounded tip relieving it of beak-like prominence. His eyelashes, thick and long from what Julia could tell with him looking downwards and them fluttering as he blinked slightly, would be a sight to behold with him in repose and them reclining just above his cheekbones. His lips, firm and thin would have been overlooked what with his blue eyes taking center stage. But they were quirked in the cutest way, kicking up at the left corner slightly as if amusement was tipping them helplessly upward. That last thought moved her from her mesmerized state and made her realize that she'd been captivated by a man, something that she never did—at least not since that marriage—and by a white man too. *That* certainly had never happened before. She'd always preferred a hint of brown.

Someone Like You
(Five Brothers: Book 3)
<u>Excerpt</u>

Nate did not hear one word the preacher said. This...this female was the most brazen, forward, and audacious woman he'd met in a long time. She was pushy and completely clueless to hints, even the most overt ones, to leave a person alone... The soft smell of baby powder intertwined with the gentle smell of roses surrounded her and hovered on the outskirts of his attention in a most tantalizing and distracting manner. Try as he might, he could not ignore her. Frustrated, Nate sighed and prayed that the Pastor was not long winded.

ABOUT THE AUTHOR

A believer in happy endings and forever after type stories, Brigette has been an avid romance reader since her teens. Inspired by her own real life romance with her husband, Clifford, she began writing romance novels after the birth of her first child and hasn't stopped since. Brigette holds a degree in Cultural Studies with a concentration in communication. Brigette writes Christian Romance and Christian Romantic Suspense. She lives in the northeastern U.S.A. with her husband and four children. She can be reached at hearthavenbooks@gmail.com or visit her website, www.brigettemanie.com. You can also find her at the links below:

http://www.amazon.com/Brigette-Manie/e/B00A3CPJC4
https://www.goodreads.com/author/show/6562932.Brigette_Manie
https://www.facebook.com/brigette.manie.author?ref=stream
https://twitter.com/BrigetteManie

CPSIA information can be obtained at www.ICGtesting.com
Printed in the USA
LVOW06s2138260715

447744LV00008B/120/P